Hannah's Vineyard

Florence Johnson

aventine press

Edited by: Shiarnice Taylor & Rose Willie

Published by Aventine Press
55 East Emerson St.
Chula Vista CA, 91911
www.aventinepress.com

ISBN: 978-1-59330-984-8

Foreword

I am so honored and excited to know Florence Johnson, to be a part of her first writing endeavor.

When I first met her, there was an immediate connection, spiritual in nature. I knew without a doubt, she was a force to be reckoned with, possessing a commanding presence when walking into a room.

The wisdom myself and others have received from Florence, comes through in the lives of her characters. Resonating to the core of her being as she pulls you into their lives; Florence leads the reader as she has led those around her.

Another world is not only possible, she is on her way. On a quiet day, I can hear her breathing... Arundhati Roy

Tonya Kelley

Dedication

I dedicate my first novel to the spirit of perseverance. The elegance of sacrifice, the gracefulness of determination and the simplicity of peace during the times of wanting to give up…yet didn't.

Chapter One

Zedekiah ceased his pacing. With one vicious stroke, he swept everything from the massive desk to the polished floor, ink spreading on the thick imported carpet. Papers fluttering and his prized ceramic globe shattering heavily against the hearth.

For a moment, Jeshurun failed to recognize his father's purposeful tirade aimed at intimidating him into seeing things his way. Jeshurun's attention torn from the hypnotic crackling of the fire was drawn to his father's commanding voice which he had been ritually ignoring.

"Father, have you…!"

"Have I got your attention now?"

"I love her, Father!" Jeshurun boldly responded, instinctively bracing himself.

"Love her indeed! "This black wench of yours is the daughter of one of my slaves!"

"Does it matter? Does it really matter?" Jeshurun stood his ground, choking back a half-plead.

"It does if you're my son."

"You're damn right it does!"

Zedekiah Fortune was intimidating not so much in size; although a man of stature, built larger than average. It was his mannerism, his booming voice and piercing dark eyes that kept those around him at bay — others cringing in fearful respect.

"This isn't getting us anywhere, Father."

Feeling the heat of the battle between them dissipating, Jeshurun simply stared at his father, determined not to give in.

"There will be no further conversation. You and your… will leave immediately." Zedekiah ceased his pacing and faced his son. "Could it be," he thought, "that Jeshurun is truly in love with that girl?" Then he said aloud, "You'll leave tonight."

"Leave? Where to, Father?"

"I've booked the two of you passage on Captain Voorheis' ship bound for the Colonies. You will set up a branch of the family business in New Amsterdam. Everything has been arranged."

"But Father!"

"Enough, Jeshurun, no more. You will leave tonight, you and…and this girl you're so in love with. If you must have her, have her you will, but not here, I wish to avoid the embarrassment."

Jeshurun looked at his father in utter disbelief. For a fleeting moment when their eyes met, Jeshurun thought he saw an intimation of compassion. Zedekiah quickly turned away, his back stiff with offense.

It was then that Jeshurun realized it was of no use to try and reason. Turning and walking away, midway across the room, Jeshurun paused once more. Turned, pleading "Father…I…"

Zedekiah turned hesitantly to respond, only to face his son's back, as he walked dejectedly away from him. A chill went up his spine as he heard the familiar voice of his deceased wife Clara, whispering… "You're a stubborn man Zedekiah Fortune."

As Jeshurun left the room, his thoughts quickly turned to Kathryn. He had to inform her of their fate. What would he say to her? He didn't dare mention to his father that she was pregnant. "My God," he thought, "will she come? Will she follow me to a strange unfamiliar place?"

Often, they had discussed the possibility of leaving, but it was only a possibility. He never thought it would happen, at least not like this or so soon.

Jeshurun made the arduous journey to the servants' quarters, dreading Kathryn's response. Finally arriving, Jeshurun knocked feebly at the door, almost wishing no one would hear and respond.

As the door slowly opened, Kathryn stood before him.

Seeing her took his breath away. Kathryn's beauty was captivating a perfect combination of features of her African father and Brazilian-Dutch mother. He loved her dark brown hair that broke in waves flowing down her back. Her hazel eyes and long lashes hypnotically drew him into her. When he was with her, looking into those eyes, nothing else mattered.

She was lithe and petite with shapely hips. Delicate to a fault. Yet he found her possessed of indomitable inner strength and power that belied her fragile beauty. If he were truly honest, it was her strength of character and spirit, which ultimately drew him to her.

"Jeshurun, what a surprise, Kathryn said."

Jeshurun gave Kathryn a half smile, not meaning to. He couldn't help it. He did his best to be brave for her sake, not wanting her to worry.

Kathryn paused for a moment, looking into Jeshurun's eyes. Something was amiss; this was not her Jeshurun.

"What is it, are you alright, she asked?"

He began to explain to her what had taken place between him and his father. "He's forcing us to leave Kathryn. I'm afraid we have no choice."

Kathryn stared at the man sitting across from her. He was so handsome, dark auburn hair, and the bluest eyes. He was muscular for an aristocrat, not having confronted much physical labor. This was her love; she was carrying his child. She would follow him to the ends of the earth. "Of course, I'll go," Kathryn said."

"You will? I had only hoped. It was so much to ask and at such short notice," Jeshurun said, tears filling his eyes. He could never love her more than he loved her at this moment.

"I promise I will take care of you, Kathryn you, and the little one."

"You better," she laughed, lightening the mood. "I'll be ready."

Kathryn closed the door after Jeshurun left. Turned and leaned against it as she closed her eyes, attempting to stop the room from spinning. Struggling to control her rapidly beating heart.

Praying that Jeshurun had not seen the concern in her eyes. She could only imagine what it must have taken for him to stand up to Zedekiah Fortune.

Calming herself, Kathryn opened her eyes only to come face to face with her mother standing in the doorway of the kitchen. Staring at her mother, it was as if the moment froze in time as mental pictures of her life flashed through her thoughts.

Marisal, Kathryn's mother, was content with her status in the Fortune household. Without complaint, she remained steadfastly loyal to the Fortune family. Marisal expected the same from her daughter.

Kathryn's mother had adamantly disapproved of Kathryn's entanglement with Jeshurun. Declaring it, more times than Kathryn could count.

Marisal, was the product of an unfortunate union of a Dutch shipping magnate and her mother an African-Brazilian slave.

Marisal's mother lived and served in the household until she became pregnant with Marisal.

Sparing the master' embarrassment, and the wrath of his wife. Marisal's mother was quickly sold at a bargain to the Fortune family.

Marisol had been given permission by Zedekiah Fortune, to marry Kathryn's father; Samuel, an African from West Africa.

Marisal's notion of destiny was vastly different from Samuel's. She could not imagine a life outside the one she knew at the Fortune's. Therefore, feared her daughters' fate.

In appearance, Kathryn took more after her mother's Dutch side. Yet her father' influence came through in other ways.

Kathryn's outward appearance contradicted her father's African genes. Nevertheless, he made certain he implanted into Kathryn ancestral stories.

His father, his mother, their village, their culture, she knew them well. Having learned their history by heart, Kathryn' father made her promise to pass the stories on to her children. She would now carry his traditions to the new world.

"Mama, I have to leave, Mama."

"Leave? Where, Kathryn?"

"Master Fortune is sending me and Jeshurun away." "We're leaving later tonight, for the British Colonies in the New World."

"N-o-o-o! No, Kathryn, I'll never see you again, or the baby!"

"What…but…, how? How did you know?"

"Why? You think you could hide such a thing from me? Are you not my flesh and blood? Samuel, Samuel, come quickly!"

"Let her go Marisal," came the booming voice of Kathryn's father, resonating through the house.

As he appeared in the doorway, his huge frame blocked the light from the room beyond. "Let her go," he repeated. "It's time, I knew this day was coming. I have prepared her for it.

Her destiny is to be fulfilled in this new land, where she is to journey. We will no longer be slaves and servants…"

"We have always been slaves, Marisal vehemently interrupted Samuel. As long as I can remember, it is all we have been and all we'll ever be."

"No, Marisal, our daughter leaves here tonight, not as a slave. As a wife. A wife of one of the richest heirs in Racife."

"It won't last. He will misuse her; we will never see her again. O-o-o, my baby!"

Kathryn watched as her father consoled her mother, then left the room, ashamed. She couldn't accept her mother's resolve that her family would always be slaves. Kathryn became angry, more resolute in her convictions.

Not only would she not be a slave, but she would make sure the child she carried would know its value and worth to be proud of its heritage.

"Marisal, as hard as it is, we must let her go, Samuel declared."

"Are you sure Samuel? Are you sure our daughter will be all right?"

"As sure as I breathe, woman. I know from the very depth of my soul, what is happening is far beyond you, me *and* Kathryn."

"What do you mean Samuel?"

"I had a dream while in my homeland of traveling to a distant land. I saw strange people speaking a language I did not know. Now, I am here in Racife.

Since being here, I have dreamed again of yet another land. In this other land, I saw my people, my ancestors, treated with great cruelty. Cruelty so much so, I could not bear to watch. Their backs were bent; their heads were low, their bodies barely clothed.

Suddenly, one by one, they began to rise above the cruelty. As they were rising, their garments began to change. They took on the appearance of those that we now serve. They were prosperous and wealthy, heads held high.

Kathryn is taking our next generation to a place of honor and prosperity. This is her and our destiny. We must allow her to fulfill it."

Kathryn' father's words resonated to the very core of Kathryn's being. Her spirit became heavy with the weight of the responsibility, of his prophetic words. Yet, the same words spoke of hope and promise.

Perhaps they might be the wishful visions of a man whose life finds hope only in dreams. Kathryn chose to believe in a greater future than of merely being the wife of a rich man.

She carried a seed that was to be planted in the soil of her father's dream, in a new land…for a new generation.

Chapter Two

New York, 1991... Hannah, having become adept at maneuvering through the subway crowd, hurried to be on time to yet another Interview. "Damn, I should have left earlier," she said disapprovingly to herself. "I pray this will not be another don't call us. We'll call you. Thank you, but not at this time. I don't think I could take another rejection."

She pondered these thoughts and many more as she entered the doors of Vineyard Corporation, making her way to the elevators. Nodding at the oblivious guard behind the information desk, Hannah entered the elevators.

Hannah began to calm herself, taking deep breaths, inhaling, exhaling. Determined to keep a positive disposition. Her goal, a self-confident, intelligent, individual, would be the perception of her interviewer. Not an anxious, apprehensive, rejected woman.

Hannah had spent a considerable amount of money, after she graduated soliciting help from an agency.

They'd practically guaranteed her a position in the best corporations; after they had groomed, fine-tuned her into their interpretation of corporate material.

Still, Hannah was unemployed, more nervous at interviews, recalling what she was or wasn't supposed to say or do. Why couldn't she just be herself? What was so wrong about being Hannah?

Hannah Lowenstan, that's who she was. She had studied hard. Worked part-time to help put herself through school.

It was finally sinking in. Her classmates had warned her, "It isn't what you know" but "who you know." Hannah was rapidly becoming a believer.

Hannah struggled with her emotions, trying to remain positive by focusing on the interview.

So many were dependent upon her, from Granmama, Uncle Ivey, a myriad of aunts, uncles, cousins, hell the whole damn community and hell was what she felt like about now. In an abyss, a place of darkness and confusion. Would she ever see the light of day to eventual success?

"Hell" was one of her favorite words these days. It helped to release the aggressive antagonistic frustration she was experiencing. Hannah believed it to be one of those expressive words she could use and stay within the confines of Granmama's raising. Every now and then she might use damn in Granmama's presence, but that was as far as she'd dare to go.

Hannah was a family first, beginning with her graduating from high school, receiving a scholarship from Radcliff. The whole community was supportive proud of her. They took up a collection at church the Sunday before she left.

Reverend Simmons had said, "It ain't much Hannah. We want you to know it is from our hearts. We want you to always remember, even if no one else does... we believe in you."

Those very words kept Hannah going when things got rough. Whenever she would have her "giving up moments." It was then she would recall his words, somehow muster the strength to keep going.

If only for those who believed in her; she refused to let them down. Staying on the dean's list, she graduated with honors. It was her way of paying them back for their sacrifices.

Family back home found it hard to believe that Hannah was not employed yet. She'd vowed not to call them until she was. To the folks back home, a college degree automatically meant you got a job, simple: one followed the other. So, they all thought, including Hannah. "How naïve we all were," Hannah voiced her thoughts aloud.

"Ok, here we are. Deep breath, relax, put on your best smile, go get that job, girl!" Hannah encouraged herself as she stepped off the elevator onto the thirtieth floor.

Searching for a receptionist, Hannah observed a woman sitting at a desk in the center of the lobby.

As she walked across the lobby, she surveyed the room. The floors were made of cream-colored marble with dark brown veins running through, speckled with gold.

There were two huge floor-to-ceiling pillars made of the same marble, with ornate wood trim at the top and bottom. Oak molding trimmed the room and windows. She had a thing for period architecture.

One summer, instead of going home, she had taken a class. The class consisted of a tour of the older buildings in and around the city.

Funny how she'd always shown an interest in things that were not normal, for a girl who grew up in a small country town. She enjoyed all kinds of music, including classical. She was an avid reader, always had been.

Reading took her places she knew that more than likely on her own, she would never get a chance to visit. Therefore, resigned herself to visiting far away exotic places through books.

Hannah's dreams were always infinite in nature, expansive. At times perplexing, and extraordinarily visionary.

Once she tried to explain a dream to Granmama. Granmama dismissed it as something Hannah had eaten, before going to bed.

After that, Hannah resolved to keep her dreams to herself. Granmama's standard of belief was just the opposite, of Hannah's. Hannah couldn't count the times granmama had said to her, "Child, your mind is too big for your pocket."

"May I help you? The receptionist queried, breaking into Hannah's reverie.

"Yes, my name is Hannah Lowenstan. I have an appointment with Mr. Roland Anderson."

While the receptionist contacted Mr. Anderson, Hannah continued with her musings, while waiting.

"Mr. Anderson will be with you shortly. Please have a seat, Ms. Lowenstan."

"Thank you," Hannah replied, taking a seat in a plush, brown, leather chair.

"Who would have thought I would have made it this far," Hannah surmised.

Hannah began to take notice of the receptionist seating area. Coffee table, two side tables, lamps and the usual montage of magazines.

As she began to peruse a Time magazine. Hannah's thoughts began to drift back home to the dusty unpaved streets where she played as a child.

Hannah had gone to live with her grandmother shortly after her mother's death. She recalled the family arguing over who did and did not want the responsibility of raising her. Granmama just stepped right into the midst of the upheaval, set things right side up and declared she would take Hannah.

Before Hannah realized what was happening, her bags were packed, and she was on a Greyhound bus headed for the town of Hadaran, South Carolina.

Strange, the things she could remember while others remained a blur.

For instance, she remembered one of Mama's male friends taking her with them on one of their dates they'd gone to the movies.

The dress she had worn was a vivid, white dress with red polka dots. Her shoes were a pair of black patent Mary Jane's with white socks. They had walked to a movie theater, not far from where they lived.

Most vividly Hannah remembered the night her mother became sick.

Mama woke up in the middle of the night sick and began vomiting. Hannah remembered running to get newspaper to place on the floor beside her bed, then called for help. The ambulance rushed mama to the hospital.

The next morning Hannah was told her mama had died. Hannah recalled, the boyfriend just disappeared, they never saw him again.

Hannah couldn't picture her mama's face, just scattered memories of different events. The funeral, memories like being too short to see over into the casket. Uncle Ivey, picking her up so she could see that was her last memory of her mother. "Man! Wouldn't a therapist have a field day with this one," Hannah thought, with a wry smile.

"Ms. Lowenstan?"

"Mr. Anderson?" A man stood in front of her extending his hand.

"I apologize for the wait."

Mr. Anderson was no surprise to Hannah. She had seen many like him after all the interviews she'd had over the past few months.

Average to well, one was good looking, real good looking; but for the most part, they were average…white, middle-aged men. Dark suits, matching ties, impeccably dressed. She speculated they must all have gone to the same stores or, stylist. They were rubber stamps of each other. Hannah recognized their type on sight, suits…exemplars of corporate America. Would she ever learn, become a member? Did she even want to?

Mr. Anderson made small talk as they walked down the hall to his office. It was the usual: "how are you. Great to meet you, how are you finding the city? What college did you graduate from or, your degree is in what? Etc.

As they entered his office, she could feel the butterflies turning flips in her stomach. His office was the best she had seen so far, and the view was fantastic. All the city between them and the Brooklyn Bridge, displayed itself grandly, beyond the floor to ceiling windows.

Mr. Anderson seated himself behind his perfectly polished antique, mahogany, claw foot desk.

Hannah studied the sculpture and books behind the glass, of a matching hutch against the wall. The hutch spanned the length of the room. Noticing her interest, he explained it wasn't a hutch at all. The cabinet had once been in a restaurant. He'd had it redesigned and custom fitted for his office. When he offered her a chair, Hannah took a silent, deep breath, the interview began.

"Well, Ms. Lowenstan, I must say I am very impressed," he stated as he stood, indicating an end to the ordeal.

"Mr. Anderson," Hannah began. Hoping the sounding rejection in her heart, had not infiltrated her voice. "When can I expect to hear from you?"

"Well, we usually background check all your information verifying your references. Then we disburse to the section managers or department heads. Whoever's interested or has an open position will get in touch."

Hannah's heart sank as she smiled at Mr. Anderson, shaking his hand firmly, as taught. Secretly wanting to tear it off at the wrist. She gathered her things headed towards the door all the while down in her belly the flipping butterflies had turned into screaming harpies that threatened to fly out clawing and screeching.

She wanted to scream! Not just scream, but to literally cuss Roland Anderson out. She wanted to ask what more he, they…anyone wanted from her?

She just wished someone would explain what exactly they wanted her to do! Was it her resume? Did she lack in interviewing skills? Wrong dress? Bad haircut? What? Why?

But she didn't she just thanked him politely, walked out hurt wounded, as usual.

Walking back towards the reception area half-dazed, Hannah felt anger filling every fiber of her being.

Somewhere from a muted background, she heard the receptionist say "good-bye" or something along those lines.

Stepping into the elevator, Hannah could feel the volcano of anger erupting with nowhere to pour itself out. As tears began to well up, her fury at the world resolved into fury at her own weakness and vulnerability.

She felt under attack by an unseen force in an incomprehensible battle for her true purpose and destiny.

Her life so far seemed like nothing more than a series of failed attempts. Yet, amid all the disappointments and despair, inside her burned a stubborn spark of determination. Persevere, what alternative was there?

Exiting the elevator, Hannah hurried across the lobby, needing to get out of the building and breathe. Nearly blinded by her tears, she failed to see the elderly gentlemen coming directly into her path. Running headlong into him, she flew one way, her portfolio and briefcase another.

That was the straw that broke Hannah's emotional back. The volcano erupted. Tears spilled over, months of frustration rejection came spewing out of Hannah, like molten lava and hot primeval gas.

Everything she ever wanted to say to those who had so smugly dismissed her including Roland Anderson rained down fire and brimstone on the unfortunate stranger.

Finally, her fire gone to ashes, she looked up into the kindest of eyes, overwhelmed by shame with embarrassment...

"Damn," expressing the emotionally charged moment the only way she knew how, "I am really sorry." "I am so sorry. You didn't deserve that." Regarding the contents of her life on the polished floor of the lobby, she touched his arm. I...this is all I need.

Hannah stooped to gather up her things, but the man interrupted reassuring her that he was just as much at fault, causing her to feel even worse. He then turned to the man accompanying him, directing him to assist Hannah in retrieving her things.

"Are you, all right?" he asked.

Hannah picked up on an intonation, it reminded her of a classmate's grandfather. She met him at a Hanukah celebration, she had been invited to.

"Yes, thank you. I am so sorry. I mean about everything I didn't mean to.

"No, no, it is I who must apologize. You must forgive the clumsiness of an old man."

"But the things I said," Hannah moaned. "I meant no disrespect. It was the frustration of a bad week. You happened to be in the wrong place, I suppose. I'm truly sorry, please accept my apology," Hannah pleaded.

"Apology accepted," he gallantly replied.

"Oh man," she thought to herself, "he's still nice and nice isn't a place I even recognize right now."

" Well Ms.?"

"Lowenstan," Hannah quipped.

"Ms. Lowenstan are you on your way out?"

"Yes," she said, really trying to be civil.

"Well, the least I can do is perhaps, offer you a ride to your destination?" He said, moving towards the exit with Hannah.

Immediately Hannah heard Granmama's warning voice, reminding her about strangers. But Hannah didn't discern a sense of warning or danger.

"I'm tired and emotionally drained, she thought. My cash is low, and the last place I want to be is on a stinking crowded subway."

Turning to the stranger, "sure, thanks."

Walking out of the building and onto the street, she was unnerved by the limo door being opened for her. Granmama's warning voice was gaining volume by the second. Knowing this could be an epic error of judgment she hesitated.

"Ms. Lowenstan?"

"Uh, yes," Hannah said, "Oh well," was her thought, Hannah entered the limo; settling deep into the far corner of the seat on full alert, followed by her elderly host.

"Tell me, what is your first name, Ms. Lowenstan?"

"My name is Hannah, she said, then thought, "Damn now he has my first name, my last name and me in the car."

"Hannah, do you know that in Hebrew, your name means "grace" or "favored," it's special. "Mine is Naboth, nice to meet you, Hannah."

"Nice to meet you too, but favored or graced is not what I'm feeling right now," "I was just turned down for the umpteenth time at my, can't count the times, interview. Don't take it personal if I don't get all aglow, about what my name means."

"In the building you were just in?" He asked.

"Yes, in the building I was just in." Hannah was embarrassed by her awful attitude, but she couldn't seem to help it.

"I was interviewed by a Roland...uh... Roland Anderson," she explained. "It was a very unpleasant interview."

Naboth unconsciously began to scrutinize the young woman seated before him, with a bit more interest. It was the first time he had been up close and personal with a person of color. Other than his long-time gentleman's companion and friend, Julius.

He'd interacted with the black employees, at board meetings, even admired some, from a distant.

To be on common ground, having to make conversation was a new experience. He didn't want to come off as being too meddlesome or too old, white, and rich. Naboth allowed the silence between them to occupy, to take the place of idle chatter.

Hannah reminded him of someone, and he couldn't recall at that moment. She was quite striking actually, despite her bad manners.

She was of fair complexion, and delicate features; high cheekbones almond shaped eyes. Full lips. A broad rounded nose, and naturally black hair testified of her black heritage. It was in one of those new styles, some kind of natural look blacks wore these days.

Some of the black executives around the office wore it. Roland tried to make a stink about it, stating that it wasn't appropriate, professional corporate attire.

He and young Williams, another of the executives had gotten into quite a dispute over it. How Naboth enjoyed seeing Williams put Roland in his place for a change.

A smile played at Naboth's lips as he thought about the incident, "m-m-m so Roland interviewed her ~ must have been for the new position in marketing. The Board wants it filled, and Roland has been dragging his feet.

I can't wait to hear what his explanation will be for turning her down. I must make a mental note to check her background and references for myself."

"Why are you staring? Hannah asked."

"Oh, was I? Sorry, seems I'm forever apologizing. I was just trying to figure out your cultural background, besides the obvious.

You see, as a matter of interest, I've been doing some research on various cultures. As of late, the interest has turned to researching about

my own family. I was just curious as to where your family were from...
I mean originally.

"I'm not sure, but strange that you would mention it, only because I
did try to do some research of my own as a project while in high school.
Not much came of it. About halfway through, I got stuck and never
completed it."

"What happened?"

"Well, all I know is there was some involvement with slavery on
Granmama's side, my mother's mother. My research before that became
complicated, too complicated for me to continue at the time. Maybe I'll
try again later. I have to admit it was quite intriguing."

"So, tell me Hannah, why were you so upset?"

She didn't answer he already knew plenty.

"Hannah, I'm genuinely concerned."

The floodgates of disappointment opened. Despite herself, Hannah
found herself sharing her entire load with this total strange ~ everything
since graduation.

"Hannah, you mustn't give up."

"Yes, I know," Hannah said, loosening up just a little, enabling her
to speak with a more courteous tongue. She even began despite herself,
to warm up to this genuinely considerate man, kind enough to share his
limo.

"But... until you find what you are looking for, may I make a
suggestion?"

"Yes, please do."

"How about coming to work for me?"

"Work for you? Doing what?"

"Well, I've needed a personal secretary and..."

"A personal what? Just hold on a minute," Hannah said, holding up
her hand in the stop position. "You honestly think I went to school all
these years to be someone's gofer secretary?"

"Please Hannah. It is not my intention to insult you. I recognize
your accomplishments. I assure you the position is legitimate. I am also
willing, because of what you've shared with me, to start you off with a
reasonable salary."

"If looks could kill, I would be dead," Naboth thought. "Boy, she's
no pushover; that's a good thing."

The word, "salary," caught Hannah's attention, snatching her back to reality. "This man is pushing my emotional buttons, she thought, "I don't even know his name. Did he tell me?"

"I don't even know your name," she said aloud.

"My name? My name is Naboth Vanderhoten, nice to meet you again, Hannah."

"What kind of reasonable salary?" She blurted.

"That's my girl," he thought. "You're smart too."

When Naboth finally gave her his offer, Hannah grabbed the armrest to keep her from falling onto the limo floor.

Fighting to keep the stunned, dumbfounded feeling from invading her face. Hannah kept repeating to herself, "poker face, poker face, poker face! Don't look desperate!"

Thank you." "All right," she said, "I'll do it, but we have to negotiate hours. I'm not willing to give up my search for a better position."

"Good, yes, of course, Hannah, Naboth agreed.

Naboth immediately liked Hannah. There was something about this young woman that spurred his interest. He was seldom ever wrong about his judgment of an individual's character, whether good or bad. "Perhaps she is the one I've been looking for. Yes perhaps," he thought.

Chapter Three

Hannah had to admit it was fun having the limo pick her up at the boarding house. As she was leaving all eyes were on her. She had shared with her roommate the events of the day, after returning, the whole house was buzzing about her job and Mr. Vanderhoten. "I wonder how that happened, she mused sarcastically." She had heard through the boarding house grapevine, some of the other girls had suggested some impropriety on her part, as if she wasn't worthy of her new-found opportunity.

Nevertheless, Hannah determined not to allow the naysayers and gossips to rain on her parade. Not even jealous, snobbish Margo who fit Granmama's favorite saying to a "t," "her mind was sure too big for her pocket." Margo was forever borrowing money in between paydays.

Amidst the whispers and catcalls, Hannah headed out the front entrance, down the steps into the street, standing at the limo door as if it were the most natural thing to do. The driver sensed what was going on, giving her a nod and a wink as he opened the door, drawing from her a smile of appreciation. She turned, entering the limo backward, sitting first then bringing her legs around mimicking the more fashionable women of the city she'd observed getting in and out of their limousines. Wow! She thought, a dream come true, only in her dream, there was a handsome man involved.

The leather was soft to the touch. In front of her was a mirrored bar with a filled ice bucket and several beverages, including water and various fruit juices. There were flowers and a note from Mr. Vanderhoten. "Very impressive," Hanna couldn't help smiling. "This is great!"

Hannah settled back, mentally preparing herself to be inundated by a million questions when she returned later. For now, she whispered, "I'm going to enjoy the ride." As the limo entered the parkway heading out of the city, Hannah allowed herself to relax, lying back, she closed her eyes. Sleep had been ephemeral last night mixed with apprehension because of her decision to work for Mr. Vanderhoten. As her thoughts drifted, they took her home.

"Hannah! Hannah! Where are you child? You hid 'in again? Bet you got your head in one of them doggone books."

A smile threaded softly across her lips, thinking how much she must have exasperated Granmama. Sneaking and hiding whenever and however she could, neglecting her chores. Either she was beginning, in the middle of, or completing one book or another. A switch was put to her behind many times. Sometimes she waited until after going to bed, then hide under the bed quilts with a flashlight, reading late into the night.

Another favorite reading spot was in the back of a long closet, next to the kitchen. The closet was filled with old clothes, some belonging to her great grandmother, the closet had a distinct smell of mothballs mingled with aged dust and rancid leftover perfume. Her grandfather's old rusted shotgun sat in a corner. When she was sure no one was looking, she would sneak in, push her way through the clothes and find a spot against the back wall, there she sat and read for as long as she could until finally the heat and profuse sweating, would drive her out. Hannah recalled how good it felt when she came out of the closet feeling the initial blast of fresh air against her face, listening cautiously before quickly tiptoeing away, before anyone saw her and discover her secret reading place.

She couldn't explain her insatiable appetite for reading, perhaps, she surmised, her books were momentary escapes, taking her on adventures, to exotic faraway places sharing in the lives of the characters portrayed. Not to mention, the wealth of information gleaned through her reading came in handy at social gatherings, while attending school.

Hannah's thoughts drifted in and out as she stared out of the window of the limo, becoming mesmerized by the scenery as it began to change. Cityscape, steel, and concrete conceding to trees and fields of wildflowers intermittently interrupted by finely manicured estates, Hannah was and always would be a country girl at heart.

The country soothed and gave sanction to her contemplative side. The side of her that was often misinterpreted as moodiness. In some instances, it energized her, inducing confidence and assurance, confirming there was nothing that she couldn't accomplish if she set her mind to it. For this reason alone, now and again she needed to go home for a visit. Visiting home slowed her down, giving her time to reflect.

"I suppose there are people who feel the same about the city," although I can't see how, she speculated, "but not me. The city and Corporate America are just steppingstones to get me where I want to be a husband, dog, cat, two kids, and a mortgage, the American dream…, yea right," Hannah chuckled.

Finally, after riding for several hours, the limo turned onto a road marked "private." Tall Junipers standing like soldiers at attention lined the road on either side. As Hannah peered through the tinted limo window, she pushed the electronic button, rolling down the window for a closer look. Behind the Junipers were rows of grapevines.

"It's a vineyard," Hannah gasped.

As far as she could see, there were row upon neat rows of grapevines. "My God, he owns a vineyard!"

After traveling for at least a quarter a mile or so, the limo came to a stop at a guardhouse adjacent to two black wrought iron gates framed by massive stone pillars. The driver stopped, got out and went into the guardhouse, then returned to the car. Suddenly the gates began to swing open. Inscrolled in an arch over the top of the gate was the name "Naboth's Vineyard."

That name sounds so familiar, she thought. Perhaps she'd read it somewhere, for the life of her, she couldn't recall why it seemed so familiar.

"There has to be acres and acres of vineyard," the vines seemed to go on forever, as far as she could see into the horizon. They were so beautiful, brilliant green leaves transparently shining in the bright July sun."

Hannah filled with amazement, remained speechless, as the main estate came into view. She had never witnessed anything so beautiful. "Breathe, that's it, breathe girl, breathe," She repeated to herself." It was as if someone had taken the most beautiful French chateau and dropped it right in the middle of a heavenly green valley then surrounded it with a vineyard. She never considered herself an emotional person, but at this very moment, she wanted to cry, thinking… people live like this, surrounded by all this beauty

Hannah began to compare the homes she had visited with college classmates.

It was during those lean financial times when she couldn't afford to go home for the holidays, various dorm mates would invite her to accompany them, so she wouldn't be left alone. Good intentions? Perhaps, Hannah would never forget going on a visit with Kara, once they arrived at her home...she revealed her true purpose for inviting Hannah... to flaunt her family's affluence no less. In spite of Kara's dishonesty, her family was very warm and inviting. But Kara's home and other homes she had visited while making their holiday rounds, paled in comparison.

Little did they know she hadn't been impressed, at least not as much as they may have assumed. Hannah muffled a chuckle as she thought of the name she'd come up with for their decorative style, "Modern Pretentious," furniture sleek and modern, kitchen chromed and outside pooled. Some of the people she met were themselves "Modern Pretentious" smooth tongued, chromed in the latest fashions, with an ostentatious air. She couldn't count the times she heard, "Why some of our best friends are black." Funny, she never saw or met any of those "black, best friends." This is not the time for cynicism, was Hannah's scolding thought, you'll want to savor every bit of this moment, before it all ends.

Chapter Four

While waiting for Hannah's arrival, Naboth followed up on her references. Deciding a background check wasn't necessary for the moment, he waited in anticipation for the last of his inquiries to respond. So far, her references were impeccable. Matter of fact, one of her professors at Radcliff had nothing but admiration for her, referring to her as "a remarkable young lady." Naboth also put in a call to Roland in an effort both to glean information and find out why he had rebuffed Hannah as a candidate for the position, Naboth became outraged thinking about the results of their conversation. It was taking him considerable effort to calm down before Hannah's arrival.

"Sir, the limo has just entered the main gate, Julius announced as he joined Naboth in the library.

"Thank you, Julius. Is everything prepared?"

"Yes, Sir."

"She didn't fit their expectations indeed!" Naboth couldn't keep from rehearsing his conversation with Roland. It played like a broken record over and over in his head.

"Calm down Naboth," he said to himself, fighting to dissipate the fire of his emotions.

He could hear the curative voice of his sister Julia she'd had an irresistible way of speaking to him when she wanted him to calm himself, after becoming angry.

"That idiot," Naboth audibly voiced his unrelenting thoughts. "How dare he lie to me. Hannah would be perfect for the new marketing position. He never intended to pursue her references. If it weren't for Julia, I would have dismissed him years ago."

Naboth always believed either intentionally or unintentionally, Roland as far as he was concerned, was chiefly responsible for his sister's death. No matter how he tried to interpret his sister's relationship with Roland, He never understood Julia's attraction to him. He speculated to the point of becoming exasperated and decided for Julia's sake, he would get along.

Roland had his ways, smooth, always the charmer, filling Julia's head with a lot of nonsensical promises. She loved him regardless.

Believed in him, trusting he would change. Unremitting in her opinion until just before her death, Julia never let on to Naboth that she had made a mistake by marrying Roland, resolving instead to make the best of it. It saddened Naboth, Julia's resolve to not allow him to share in her pain.

Towards the end of her illness, her sorrow for her children was wretchedly obvious. Many of her and Naboth's conversations ultimately lead to her advocating for their portion of her inheritance. He had bequeathed Julia a portion of Vineyard, she was family. Julia had been his encourager and support from the very beginning, no brother and sister could be closer than he and Julia.

Julia knew her children well, aware of their penchant for leaning towards the weak character and behavior of their father, he and Julia fought over the need for her to exercise more discipline in their lives instead of catering to their every whim,

Julia's concern leaned more toward Sylvia and Saul the two eldest, less for David, the youngest. He was more like his mother. Sylvia was spoiled and manipulative, Saul wanted everything for doing nothing. Naboth had tried to encourage Saul to come into the business and work alongside him, but he had always resisted. Naboth believed Roland was the source of conflicts between him and Saul.

Doctors could not fully explain Julia's death. She had been struggling with a viral infection that had attacked her lungs, but it wasn't an illness that should have caused her demise, according to Doctor Shapiro. He had hinted more than once, that it was more psychological than physiological. She had simply given up, refusing to fight the illness.

Naboth recalled, it was a week after an article regarding Roland and one of his shameless socialite friends had hit the society page that Julia passed. From sorrow no doubt, Naboth voiced his deep-seated secret aloud. From that point on he vowed that Roland would gain no more access to Vineyard Corporation than what he had through his marriage to Julia. He was well aware of office gossip regarding Roland's antics behind his back. His comments of being "next in line" and "the old man" not being what he used to be, was well known. He never trusted Roland; he certainly didn't trust him now.

Naboth hated the bitterness that ate at him. It was not in his character to feel this way. He'd tried hard at times to be cordial to Roland as well as his niece and nephews. God help me to find some peace, he mumbled to himself.

"Sir."

"Yes."

"Ms. Lowenstan has arrived. The limo is just pulling into the drive."

"Thank you, Julius."

"Julia, how I miss you, my dearest," sighing with grief Naboth thought about Julia and his last conversation. He'd refused to back down as she pleaded with him to make promises, he knew he could not keep, promises concerning Roland. He swore Roland would never get Vineyard Corporation— never, he would see it destroyed first. But... for the sake of peace between them, he compromised and kept Roland on at Vineyard as well as bequeathing a substantial inheritance for his niece and nephews.

Dissension in his family caused Naboth anguish. His concept of family was entrenched and rooted in ancestral history. He had become obsessed with his family tree. The research that started as a hobby to console him after Julia's death had taken him from his ancestral land of Israel to Holland around the sixteenth century. What surprised him was what he found after Holland. He chuckled to himself, thinking what a shock it would be to Mr. Roland Anderson, but he had more research to do to be sure.

Meanwhile, he was keeping everything to himself, hopeful that the results would resolve his current dilemma an heir for Vineyard.

Cultural tradition dictated that the family inheritance must never leave his family; it must be passed down from one generation to the other. This ingrained belief haunted him, he fervidly believed he was bound to it. "Leave it to Roland... never! Naboth whispered through clenched teeth." "But, who? He thought, who?

This question weighed upon him like an ominous dark cloud, until he spent nights tossing and turning only to wake the next morning, exhausted. His doctor had warned him on more than one occasion that he needed to eliminate stress from his life, whatever the causes and learn to relax. He'd be damned before he'd allow Roland to get his hands on his and Julia's dream, their years of sacrifice and labor demanded that Vineyard be passed on to a worthy heir.

Hannah hesitated before ringing the doorbell, her emotions fluttering in her chest as she desperately tried to calm and compose herself. Before she could do either, the door opened. Standing before her was the biggest, blackest man she had ever seen. He had to be all of seven foot, she surmised, huge hands, a chest like an ox, dressed in a butler's uniform, "he wasn't ugly just big," she thought, Hannah gasped, dumbfounded, finally after what seemed an eternity, he spoke.

"Ms. Lowenstan, I presume?"

"Yea uh yes, I-I-I mean, yes I am," she stammered.

"I'm Julius."

"Julius?" Hannah thought, "Lurch is more fitting, as she recalled the character on the T.V. show The Adams Family. At least a name within that category... but Julius?"

"I'm Hannah," she finally said.

"Mr. Vanderhoten is expecting you. Follow me, Miss."

"You can call me Hannah, she answered.

She surmised, "May as well get friendly upfront. I may need this brother." The thought drew a chuckle from her.

"What do you do for Mr. Vanderhoten," she asked.

"I'm a gentleman's gentleman. I make sure Mr. Vanderhoten's life runs as smooth as possible. When necessary, I act as his bodyguard," Julius replied.

Hannah stopped listening at the word "bodyguard." She wondered why Mr. Vanderhoten would need a bodyguard. Her imagination began to take flight, "ok, Hannah, slow it down. Come back to earth. Lots of rich people have bodyguards for one reason or another, nothing to get uptight about. Still she thought, it makes me wonder."

As they continued down a long hallway, Hannah couldn't help but sneak a peek into each room as they passed, each one seemingly more beautiful than the next. "I wonder who decorated," she pondered "surely not him. Bet there's a female somewhere in the picture. M-m-m-m can't picture that either, not that he's ugly or unattractive. He's handsome in a rich corporate sort of way, meaning money and status has a way of lending the appearance of being handsome." Chuckling out loud, she unintentionally gained Julius's attention.

"You find something humorous, Ms. Lowenstan?"

"Uh...no, I was just..."

To her relief, they arrived at what seemed to Hannah to be a combination library office. As they entered, Hannah barely heard

Naboth's greeting. She stared open-mouthed in awe. Never had she seen so many books in someone's home. She thought the little collection she had growing up was something, but this…

"Ms. Lowenstan, how nice to see you again. Did you have a pleasant trip?"

"Yes, Thank you. It was beautiful," Hannah answered distractedly, trying to read book titles and return Naboth's greeting at the same time.

"Well, come right in and we'll get started."

"Started?"

"I took the liberty to set out coffee and pastries. Have you had breakfast?"

"No, but thanks, I'm too nervous to eat."

"Well, perhaps later. Shall we?" he said, offering her a seat in front of his desk.

After what seemed like hours, Hannah stretched. Confidence soared as she went head to head with Naboth, discussing various projects and marketing strategies.

"Mr. Vanderhoten?" Julius interrupted at the door of the library.

"Yes, Julius."

"Mr. Scott is here to see you."

"Ready for a break, Hannah? I ordered lunch to be served out in the garden. There's a washroom down the hall if you need to freshen up. If you'll excuse me, I'll join you later," Naboth said, rising from his chair.

"Sure."

Hannah headed in the direction Naboth had pointed out to her, humming in blissful contentment, satisfied that she was just as much a contributor to the discussion as Naboth. It was so important to her that she not disappoint her benefactor.

She smiled to herself, not being able to help it. She was finally utilizing what she had worked so hard at learning. Everything that had happened since graduation was beginning to occupy her thoughts. For weeks she had been experiencing a stirring, a desire to walk into her purpose in life. She'd felt like a woman who had been in labor for months. Only she has been waiting to deliver creative dreams and ideas. It's been so frustrating, at least until now. Naboth had challenged her in ways that drew her to her birthing point, and now she was ready to break forth. He had even given her, her first assignment, asking that she work out all the particulars, come back with her suggestions.

After spending the morning with Naboth, she was more relaxed, believing she had a true friend and mentor. He was an excellent teacher. Patient, yet one who would not accept anything less than excellence from her. Hannah needed this. It brought out the best in her.

Not having found anything that even looked remotely like a bathroom, Hannah was becoming frustrated while opening and closing doors. In the distance, she heard muffled voices and headed toward the sound. Naboth was talking to a man, presumably the reason for their break. Naboth looked up.

"I'm sorry, Hannah interrupted apologetically, "but I seem to be lost. I can't find the washroom."

"My apologies, Hannah. I'm afraid in my haste perhaps I wasn't very clear with the instructions. Go back two rooms. It's the third door on your left."

Hannah apologized again and walked back in the direction from which she'd come wondering why Naboth hadn't introduced her to his guest.

Reaching for the correct doorknob, Hannah froze, staring at a portrait on the wall. She could have sworn she was looking at Great Granma Lizzie. "My God," she thought, "if I didn't know better…well everyone has a twin somewhere. I'll have to look at the family pictures the next time I'm at home."

Hannah washed up, preparing for lunch, thinking about the morning. She was finding it hard to believe that she was truly living in this moment. Physically present in her dreams, as they were being manifested.

She still didn't know much about Naboth except that he was the founder and CEO of a major corporation." I need to find out which one, even at the risk of sounding suspicious. The salary is excellent, so I intend to give the position my all. But my plan is not to be a personal secretary for the rest of my life. I don't care how good the money is. I didn't spend the past eight years in school to do this. My dream is to be a top executive in a major corporation someday, maybe my own, who knows?"

Chapter Five

Hannah walked through the French doors leading to the garden. Lying before her was a feast for the eyes: perfectly manicured hedges and lawn interspersed with flowers that she could not begin to name or identify. The various flowers so close together were distinguishable only by the differences in color, size, and shape. The roses alone took her breath away. "Who is this man, and what have I gotten myself into?" she asked herself pensively.

"Oh, Hannah, there you are. I apologize for the misunderstanding earlier," Naboth said.

"That's okay. I found it. I can't get over this garden. It's beautiful."

"Well, there's a little history behind it. If you would like, we can take a walk through it later, and I'll share it with you."

"Yes, I'd like that very much."

"So, Hannah, were you able to come up with any suggestions for the project I gave you?"

The two of them casually walked toward a gazebo in the center of the garden, a floral fragrance emanating the atmosphere as they walked the cobblestone path, sending her senses into delightful delirium.

"I've made a few mental notes, she responded. I'll have more later, but to make the assessment complete and more accurate, an on-site visit would be necessary. Since that is not possible, I promise to do the best I can."

"Why is that not possible?"

"I would have to or should talk to the managers and the employees. If I'm going to get a complete perspective, I need to hear from them too. There are people and lives involved. You just can't make across the board decisions without getting the whole picture. You of all people should know that," she asserted.

"Naboth laughed at his passionate protégé. "The whole picture indeed," Naboth exclaimed, rivaling her passion. "Then go you will."

"Go?" Hannah asked in utter disbelief. "Me?"

"Yes, you."

"I thought you just wanted me to do the initial work and planned to send someone else. You're talking about, what-four or five different sites? Once I complete my initial assessment. I would have to evaluate each one. Do some projections… it's going to take at least several weeks just to prepare Naboth. That's a lot of travel time and I…"

"Hannah, did you not say it was necessary in order to do a complete and comprehensive evaluation?"

"Well, yes, but…"

"Then you will. We have time. I'll work with you a while longer until you fill comfortable with what you've done. By then, you'll know exactly which stores you must visit. You'll do fine."

Naboth and Hannah entered the mansion through the lanai. Hannah walked as if in a daze, still trying to comprehend the extent of what they had just discussed. He was sending her. She sat, eating in slow motion, hardly noticing the beautifully decorated table. Everything impeccably laid out, from the centerpiece to the china and silverware. It was as if where she was, what was just presented to her, was not connecting with her personal reality.

She never dreamed that something like this… no, then again, that's just it, she did dream. But her dreams were always clouded with Granmama's constant philosophical reminders not to get the big head. She knew in her heart Granmama meant well, but some of the things she said to her had taken its toll on her self-esteem and confidence. Hannah constantly battled with maintaining both, throughout her college years. It was hard to understand Granmama's placing so much emphasis on education, at the same time, placing limits on what Hannah should or should not aspire to be in life.

Even after accomplishing what she had so far, in her heart, there was always a hint of doubt. She was constantly second guessing herself. 'Would she,' 'could she,' and 'what ifs' always interceded. Adding to that, the daunting sick need to be validated.

Hannah loathed that part of herself more than anything. It seemed as if she'd been fighting all her adult life to overcome her need for self-validation. Somehow despite Granmama's intentions, she resolved to accept it as Granmama's way of keeping her grounded, not prideful. Intentional or not, it filled Hannah with insecurities that she was at odds with every day, trying to keep them at bay. Telling herself to reach for the moon, and perhaps catch a star along the way.

"Now look at you, she said to herself, sitting here in this beautiful garden. Not to mention this awesome mansion. A total stranger, paying you a six-figure salary, now adding travel, really Hannah!

Ok, this has got to be a joke, she argued with herself. Someone saw me coming. No, I know, I've got it. My former classmates are playing a cruel, sick joke on me. This is not real," she thought.

"Hannah!" "Are you all right, Naboth asked, noticing a strange look clouding her face?"

Hannah's head snapped back, startled from the sudden sound of her companion's voice, realizing she was not alone, Hannah responded muttering...

"Oh, I'm sorry Naboth. Yes, I'm fine. It's just all so overwhelming. I suppose I'm beginning to question some things."

"Like what?"

"My being here for one," Hannah said. "I keep asking myself why you chose me? Is this real, and when is the bomb going to drop?"

"Well, Hannah, I don't know about any bomb, but I can assure you that on my part, I am totally sincere about your position here. I hope eventually to share some things with you to confirm how sincere I am. But *you,* young lady must at least give me the benefit of a doubt. I can and do recognize that you are a very gifted and talented young woman, whom I'm glad to have in my employ.

"Oh, wow, he's won me over. There's that sick validation. He recognizes my gifts and talents," Hannah thought, unable to hold back an acquiescence smile. "Damn, it's definitely not the time for suspicious questions. They'll keep until another time."

"All right," Hannah said, "I'll stay. I'll get the information together and have it ready as soon as possible."

"Take your time Hannah. We'll work together," Naboth said assuring.

Chapter Six

Hannah yawned and stretched looking around. The room looked different in the daylight than it did last night. She felt like a princess. All that was needed to complete her fantasy was for her lady-in-waiting to come in. The plush bed was a welcome relief from the cot-sized twin bed at the boarding house. She had worked until early evening. After sharing with Naboth her concerns regarding her position. She'd argued with him profusely about spending the night. Even though she felt she was being overly suspicious, she couldn't help it. Granmama had done her job well. Hannah considered herself open minded and part of the new thinking generation but spending the night in a house with a strange man she hardly knew was pushing it. However, as Naboth said...

"This mansion is so big she could occupy one side and he the other, and ne'er the twain would meet."

When she returned to the boarding house the next day to pick up her things, it was hard explaining her decision to everyone. She'd even came close to slapping her roommate. The more she explained, the more it sounded as if she was doing something unethical; so eventually, she stopped trying. Packed her things and leaving as quickly as possible. However, leaving in the limo didn't help her case of ethics and principles.

Mrs. Davis had a fit, "What will your grandmother think? Have you thought this through, Hannah?"

Hannah did her best to reassure Mrs. Davis that she would be all right, telling her she would call and give her a contact number if that would make her feel better. Hannah chuckled, realizing it wouldn't be a bad idea. Also, a wise one. J-u-s-t in case she was moving in with Dr. Jekyll and Mr. Hyde.

But a confidant voice deep in her heart spoke differently. She recalled her and Naboth's walk through the garden. Listening to him as he shared the story of his sister's dedication to designing and planning each section of the garden how each section represented a milestone in their lives. The roses with their thorns represented the beginning years of the business. Difficult and painful as they were, their hard work eventually produced, like the roses, a sweet fragrance of success.

He'd also explained the portraits on the hallway wall. Not sure how he would receive her comment, Hannah decided not to mention that one of them reminded her of one of her family members.

Hannah would always remember the love and tenderness she heard in his voice when speaking of his sister. Therefore, she concluded, among other things, Naboth was safe. When she arrived back at the mansion, she decided to stop her incessant reasoning. After working on her project for a while, she was able to go to bed less anxious.

．．．．

The next morning Hannah quickly dressed and headed downstairs to meet Naboth for breakfast. When she entered the dining room, she spoke to Julius, who grunted in return.

"Good Morning Naboth," she said.

"Good morning, Hannah. Did you sleep well?" he replied.

"Fairly well. I think it's being in a strange place. It's going to take some time getting used to my surroundings. Naboth, I have that report."

"Not now, Hannah. I make it a habit not to do business while dining. I don't believe in business breakfast', lunches or dinners. Food is a pleasurable experience and should represent a time of relaxation and the enjoyment of one's companions, whoever they are." "We'll have plenty of time to go over your report. Enjoy your breakfast, Hannah. Don't be so uptight," Naboth directed.

Hannah wanted so much to impress Naboth. She had worked long into the night and then got up early to complete the project. She felt content she had done her best. "How dare he call me 'uptight' if that's not the pot calling the kettle black!" she quipped, amused with herself.

"I still want to pinch myself," Hannah thought. "I can't believe this is happening. One minute I am stressing about how, or will I ever find employment. Now I'm working on a project that will take me across the country as an executive determining the outcome of five major department stores. At least that's what I've broken it down to so far. There's something strange about the whole thing if you ask me. I just can't figure it out. Given all the facts, it doesn't seem right. Why would these stores be running below profit level? Well, I'll see eventually."

"Naboth, I need to know what time you would like to meet today." Before we do, I'd like to make a few phone calls. I'm afraid some will be long distance I want to let Granmama know where I am and give her a number in case of emergency."

"Of course, Naboth heartily agreed." "I wouldn't want your grandmother to worry. I must go into the office today; I've been away for several weeks. It's time I made an appearance. There are some things that require my personal attention. You just relax, enjoy yourself. Familiarize yourself with the house, and I'll see you at dinner."

"All right. Are you sure?"

"Yes, Hannah, please relax. It's okay."

Hannah thought, "If he tells me to relax one more time, I'll scream. Maybe I am a little uptight, but it's only because I don't want to give him the impression that I'm taking advantage of his generosity. I'm here to work, and that's what I want to do."

"All right, Mr...I mean, Naboth. I'll go call Granmama. Have a good day, I'll see you at dinner."

Naboth shook his head, smiled, thinking, "Yes, I do like her, I do indeed. A little grooming and she's going to be great.

"Julius," Naboth called over the intercom.

"The car has been brought around Sir."

"Thank you, Julius."

"Julius met Naboth at the front door, Julius?

Yes, sir."

"Make her feel welcome. Make her feel good about being here."

"Sir?"

"Hannah, I truly believe she's going to be good for us, for our family."

"Yes, Sir, I'll do my best."

"I know you will. I've always been able to count on you. Good day, Julius."

"Good Day, Sir." Julius stood for a moment watching Naboth walk to the car. He hadn't seen Naboth so animated since Julia's death. "He wondered. Who is this Hannah person, and why has she stirred up so much hope and energy in Naboth? Yes, I *will* get to know her; I will get to know her indeed."

• • • •

Julius had been in Naboth Vanderhoten's employ for over forty years. Since Julia's death, he has been more protective of Naboth than usual. He made sure his niece and nephews didn't take advantage of him by any means, especially Sylvia, his niece.

Speech dripping with honey, talk like she loves him to death, the death part yes, love, well, that was questionable. Neither did he like Sylvia's fiancé Nesbitt. There was something about him that made his skin crawl. "With a name like Nesbitt," Julius chuckled to himself. Regardless of how well dressed or how many degrees he had, Julius made it a point to watch him like a hawk whenever he and Sylvia came around. Now, he thought displeased, I have to deal with this Hannah girl. Showing up seemingly out of the middle of nowhere. Julius made a mental vow to himself, "I'll get to know her alright. "I'll get to know her really well.

Chapter Seven

Hannah dreaded calling Granmama because of the questions she knew granmama would overwhelm her with. She'd put it off for as long as possible, becoming more apprehensive the longer she waited. Not to mention, Granmama could call the boarding house at any time and find out she was no longer there. That, she didn't need.

She rehearsed over and over what she would say, knowing full well Granmama was not going to understand why she was living with some strange white man she hardly knew. Maybe she wouldn't tell her she was living with him; she would only say she was now employed. Any further explanation would be given to Granmama, face to face.

Hannah slowly dialed the number. "Hey, hi Granmama!"

"Hannah? That you Baby?"

"Yes, Granmama, it's me. How are you doing? Are you taking care of yourself?"

"Oh, yes, best I can. Ain't much else to do but take care of myself."

Hannah sighed, "Here it comes."

"You working yet?"

Granmama didn't take long to ask the proverbial question Hannah knew was coming.

"Yes, Mam. As a matter of fact, I am Granmama."

"Oh, you are? Wait until I tell Ivey. He'll be glad to hear that, and so will everyone else. We were getting' worried bout you, how you were makin' out. That's good Hannah, really good."

"I know, Granmama. You all should stop worrying, I'm employed now. Got a good position. I'm fine."

"So, tell me, what are you doing?"

"Oh man," Hannah thought, "what am I going to tell her? I can't lie to Granmama."

"I'm a consultant. When a corporation is experiencing trouble, I find out what the problem is and offer a solution," Hannah answered. "There, that ought to do it," Hannah concluded to herself.

"Is it good money?"

"Very good Granmama, I'll also do some traveling."

"I'm so proud of you Baby."

"Thanks, Granmama. Tell Uncle Ivey, 'Hello' for me. I'll see you all soon. Granmama?"

"Yes, Hannah?"

"Remember those pictures of Great Grandma Lizzie I used for my history project?"

"Yes, what about them?"

"You still have them?"

"Of course, I do, Baby. Why wouldn't I?"

"Nothing, I just wanted to know so I could look at them when I come home for a visit. I was thinking about it the other day. I'll talk to you again soon. Love you."

"Love you too, Baby. Bye."

"Bye, Granmama."

Hannah hung up the phone, hoping Granmama accepted what she had said. She hated being deceitful with Granmama, to this day she couldn't tell an outright lie to Granmama. Her roommate at college teased her a lot because she was forever in trouble with girls in the dorm, the guys, and her professors because she was "too honest."

After hanging up the phone with Hannah, Granmama wasn't quite sure what to think. She knew Hannah too well. Hannah was holding out on her, but she wasn't sure what it was, something in her voice. "Oh, well," she thought, "I'll find out after a while. I always do. I just hope my child's all right."

"Ivey! Ivey! Hannah's finally got a job! She's working now!"

Hannah had to make one more phone call. To Asah. No one really knew for certain what kind of relationship her and Asah had. Folk talked perhaps had their suspicions and suppositions, but no one really knew. Asah was married and much older than Hannah. They had kept their friendship as discreet as possible, which was almost impossible in a town the size of Hadaran.

Hannah came to know Asah through his friendship with her Uncle Ivey. At the time he was separated from his wife, Hattie. She was fifteen when they first became "intimate" in a friendship sort of way. She saw nothing wrong with them being friends. Their friendship grew over the years. He had always been there for her, she could depend on him, and she valued his advice.

Hannah could talk to Asah about things she wouldn't dare approach with Granmama. He had helped her through a very traumatic experience, one Hannah avoided thinking about as much as possible. Whenever she did think about it, she'd call her Aunt Aria. "Odd she thought, it's been a while since I've heard from Aria. I hope it's because…never mind I don't want to think of that right now."

Turning her thoughts back…Asah, sweet Asah, he'd been there through it all. The gap in their ages never seemed to matter, twenty some odd years. He'd gleaned from her youthful wisdom. She from him, mature answers for her questions to life's dilemmas. She knew he'd never leave Hattie. Not that she would ever want him to. He was a man of principle. Said he would keep his marriage vows to the end. Anyway, he told her once, "I'm too old to start all over again."

Asah had made a good life for himself and Hattie. He wasn't an educated man, but he had worked hard for many years to gain domestic and financial stability. He couldn't just walk away from either. Hannah would never forget their last night together just before she left for college. Her heart quickened as she closed her eyes for a moment to re-live that night. Tears began to find their way to the surface at just the thought of him. He would never know how much he meant to her, and she could never let him know.

"Asah?"

"Hey! How's my girl?"

"I'm fine," she said grinning from ear to ear at the sound of his voice.

"You okay? Nothing's wrong, is it?"

"No, as a matter of fact, I have good news, I'm working."

"You are? That's great!"

Hannah began to explain what had transpired over the past few weeks, knowing she could tell Asah.

"Are you sure you're going to be all right?" he asked.

Hannah could hear the concern in his voice.

"Yea, I'm fine. He better not try anything, "she laughed. "I miss you."

"I miss you too, Angel. Stay in touch."

"You call me sometimes too," Hannah reminded him.

"Ok."

"Bye, Asah," Hannah said, hanging up the phone, sinking deeply into the plush leather chair.

Hannah jumped, startled by a noise from behind her. Who's there?" she yelled, trying not to sound frightened. Scanning the room, she slowly made her way to the door. Stepping timidly through the doorway, peeping around the corner, she screamed. It was Julius.

"What are you doing? You scared me half…half…to death!" she stammered.

"I'm sorry, Ms. Lowenstan," he replied.

"I'll bet you are," Hannah snapped. "Do you always go around sneaking up behind people?"

"Sneaking?"

"Yes, sneaking!"

"I have no reason to sneak, Ms. Lowenstan."

"Wasn't that you behind me just now?"

"No, Mam."

Hannah mentally checked herself, remembering she wanted to glean information from Julius about Naboth. She could not afford to make him her enemy.

"Never mind," Hannah conceded.

"I've got to keep a close eye on Mr. Julius," she thought.

• • • •

Asah was glad to hear from Hannah. For years he'd struggled with the desire to reveal to her his true feelings but would not knowing it wouldn't be fair to her. He was after all a very married man. He and Hannah had grown close during his and Hattie's separation. Anyway, he'd always thought Hannah saw him merely as a father figure and confidante.

But the night before Hannah went off to college, changed his mind. He realized she didn't think that way at all. He knew she wanted him, and he wanted her more. However, he couldn't bring himself to take from her the only thing she had left to give to him other than her friendship and her love…herself. He decided he couldn't take from her what he wasn't able to give back, himself. He wasn't free to do that, and Hannah didn't deserve anything less. She could never know how much she meant to him, and he would never let her know.

Chapter Eight

Naboth used the opportunity of the ride into the city to make phone calls, ordering and sorting out minutiae prior to his arrival at the office. Specifically, he wondered about Roland and his decision not to hire Hannah. Naboth was hard-pressed to figure out how to address the situation without letting Roland know Hannah was under his employ. He wasn't ready just yet to reveal her to anyone. Why? he wasn't sure, he just felt it necessary, to keep Hannah under wraps for a while longer.

Upon arrival at the office, Naboth decided to enter unannounced through a little-known passageway. It was a series of corridors between two walls adjacent to an old service elevator. He'd had it designed for the express purpose of keeping staff from knowing when he was in. Julia called it 'being sneaky and spying.' He called it 'good managerial sagacity.' How else would he know what his staff was really up to when he wasn't around?" It also allowed him to give Roland the occasional slip. Only his personal secretary knew when he was in or out, and he could depend on her confidentiality. Naboth pressed the release button that opened a door in the wall just behind his desk.

The walls in his office were made of teak paneling. The furniture consisted of two dark brown leather chairs and a sofa. The sofa was custom made to fit the length of the wall. High on one wall was a recessed bookshelf with glass doors and below that a cabinet housing a sink and refrigerator. A small pantry stocked with amenities for late night business meetings, a closet with several suits, ties, shoes, for overnight stays at the office.

The window in his office was what he considered his only reckless expense. It filled both the breath and height of the room, looking out over the city and beyond. It gave the sense of being outdoors, not confined. He allowed himself this luxury because he spent so much of his time here.

. . . .

"Cynthia?"

"Yes, Mr. Anderson."

"Is the old man in yet?"

"I haven't seen him as of yet, Roland."

"Well, all right. Let me know when he arrives, will you?"

"Yes Sir, as soon as I hear from him."

Roland was anxious, more nervous than usual. He didn't have a very good night. Cybil had continued to hound him about marriage. She refused to accept the fact that he could not make a commitment right now. It wasn't good timing. Naboth had been pressuring him to sell his and Julia's share back to the corporation, and they were still in negotiations. To announce an engagement or to marry at this point would be financial suicide, even if it had been almost two years since Julia's death. The controversy behind Julia's death made it impossible for Roland to make the kind of commitments Cybil demanded. No, last night had not been good at all. "Damn, where is Naboth?" Roland said to himself.

Naboth called his secretary to inform her of his arrival. Sarah immediately went in to get his instructions for the day. Sarah's lifelong relationship with Naboth created a familiarity of his likes and dislikes, a routine of sorts. Entering his office, she said, "Your tea, with milk, lemon and honey, and your messages and mail, Sir." "It's good to see you in the office today, you've been gone for a few weeks, you ok?"

Naboth replied, "Please, Sarah. you don't have to call me Sir." "We've known each other for far too many years."

"Not here at the office...sir, Sarah replied with a sarcastic smile." "Roland has been chomping at the bit, waiting to see you. He's called several times, inquiring as to your whereabouts."

"Keep him waiting a little longer for me, will you Sarah? Let me get my bearings first."

"Yes Sir, will do."

"Sarah?"

"Yes."

"I appreciate you."

Sarah, closing the door behind her, "Thank you kind sir."

Sighing deeply Naboth sipped his tea, perused his mail then leaned back in his chair in deep concentration.

He trusted Sarah, trusted her with his very life. She had been wonderful throughout Julia's illness and pretty much ran the office during the last few months prior to her death. If anyone deserved to be his replacement, she did. But Sarah had always told him she was not CEO material and had no inclination or desire to be.

At some point or another, Naboth reminded himself, I'm going to have to introduce her to Hannah. H-m-m-m, I wonder how Hannah's doing. I must remember to call and check on her today.

"Sarah?" Naboth called over the intercom.

"Yes," Sarah said appearing in the doorway,

"Let's get this over with," Naboth said with an agitated look. "You may send Roland in."

. . . .

"Naboth, my boy!" Roland said, striding into the office.

"Roland."

"I've been waiting to see you, old man."

"I've asked you time and time again not to call me that, Roland."

"Oh, I thought you only meant when we were in mixed company, surely not when it's just you and I?"

"Not at all, Roland."

"As you wish."

"How are you coming along with filling that position in marketing?"

"I've had some bites but nothing substantial."

"Roland, that position is crucial. We must get it filled immediately. I was told you've had several interviews, one as recent as last week."

"Yes, but none were qualified."

"Let's do this. Bring all of the resumes of the people you have interviewed to the ten o'clock board meeting."

"That won't be necessary, Old Man. Oops, old habits are hard to break. Surely you don't think that is necessary, Naboth."

"Roland, the board gave you this assignment six months ago, and the position is still vacant. Maybe you could use some input and suggestions from the board to assist you with the process. We'll go over the qualifications and review some of the applicants. Was there anything else, Roland?"

Roland could barely maintain his composure as he left Naboth's office, mumbling, "How dare he suggest I was incompetent." I know it's been a while, but I've had a lot on me lately. Julia's death and my relationship with Sybil have been stressful, to say the least. I wish he'd get off my back. Then to add injury to insult, he brings up his buyout offer. Naboth is pushing it," he muttered through clenched teeth.

Sarah looked up as Roland came storming out of Naboth's office. As she opened her mouth to speak Roland's countenance and fast paced exit indicated she should probably keep her obligatory remarks to herself. 'Have a good day, Mr. Anderson,' she murmured softly. "M-m-m-m, I wonder what that was all about."

Naboth breathed a sigh of relief after his meeting with Roland had come to an end. A smile played at the corners of his lips as he thought about Roland's reactions, "If Roland only knew just how close Hannah really is."

The board meeting went well. All had agreed that Roland had two weeks to decide on one of three applicants. Naboth had intentionally left Hannah's application out because he wanted to keep her right where she was. Naboth had plans for Hannah. Plans as in the vernacular of today's youth, "that would blow her mind?" She'd sounded excited when he spoke with her prior to the board meeting. Said she had the proposal ready for his review upon his return. It felt good to have her around. It was like having Julia back again.

Naboth put in a call to inform Sarah of his departure.

"Leaving so soon?" Sarah said, surprised at his early departure. "This is unusual, a meeting?"

"No, Sarah, just some personal business I need to take care of. If anyone asks, tell them I'm gone for the day."

"Yes…uh…well… all right, have a good evening." "I hope he's not sick." Sarah thought, becoming a little concerned. "It's not like him to be so secretive."

Naboth knew Sarah would be concerned, he wasn't usually so secretive with her. But Hannah had to be kept confidential for the time being. He needed to explain things to Hannah first. Things like, he is the founder and CEO of Vineyard, Roland was his brother-in-law, and why he had kept all of this from her. Hopefully in time, Hannah would come to understand his decision to wait.

Naboth decided before leaving the city, to stop by Mr. Scott's office to check on his progress since the last time they met. The very thought of finding a relative gave Naboth goosebumps. According to their last conversation, Scott was making progress. Just thinking about the possibilities was encouraging, to say the least. His concerns would be alleviated finally giving him peace, knowing Vineyard would have an heir. Until then, he took some comfort in having the good fortune of having Hannah enter his life, at just the right time.

Naboth was aware of his penchant to fall into bouts of hopelessness. Normally he would confide in Sarah. She was more than just his secretary. Over the years she had become his confidante, his friend. But for some reason, whenever he tried to talk with her about his search for his ancestral heritage, she looked at him with that enigmatic look of hers; he could never understand that look! He just decided to keep that part of his life to himself. As of late, he stopped confiding in Julius too. He felt until he had something more substantial, he'd wait before sharing with anyone again.

Chapter Nine

Hannah had spent most of the morning polishing off the proposal for Naboth. She was pleased with herself. She was able to identify at least three sites that were in trouble. They were the ones she'd determined were necessary to visit before making her conclusive analysis.

What she found strange while doing her research was the appearance of the same name a Mr. Anderson. Apparently, he was the key person and someone for intuitive reasons she questioned. Strangely enough, no one had ever met him. It was as if he was some kind of corporate apparition. Yet he held all the decision-making power. The managers she spoke with were only able to give her information that was sketchy at best. And whenever they'd tried to get in touch with this phantom Mr. Anderson, they were sent through the proverbial 'corporate' evasion maze, of passing the buck. Finally exasperated they gave up. Naboth would know, she deduced.

Hannah decided to take a break. She was famished, realizing she hadn't eaten all day. Rising from her chair, she stretched looking around the library, wondering when she would ever have the luxury of cuddling up with a good book. Smiling teasing herself, she thought, "reading or working young lady." Laughingly she said, working of course," and headed down the hall towards the kitchen.

Hannah had spent some time earlier, wandering through the main house in an effort to familiarize herself with the premises. She could have sworn that her every move was being watched. She'd presumed it was Julius watching out for Naboth's interest. Concluding, it was the appropriate thing for him to do. "Once Julius is assured, I mean Naboth no harm, I'm hoping he'll be just as protective of me," she reasoned. The very thought caused Hannah to smile, humming as she walked.

"Now, what is she smiling about," Julius thought. "I didn't get a damn thing done today, trying to keep an eye on her, that girl was all over this house.

I'm too old for this. Maybe she's all right, but I've got to be sure, for Naboth's sake. Miss Julia made me promise to take care of him. I'll be glad when he gets home. Looks like she's headed for the kitchen. I'd better beat her there." Julius thought. Knowing every room, doorway, secret hideaways, and passages he'd easily get there ahead of her.

When Hannah entered the kitchen, Julius stood at the massive restaurant style stove. It's stainless steel hood sparkling, having been shined to perfection as were the copper pots and cooking utensils hanging from hooks on a pot rack extending from the ceiling. Everything was immaculately clean. Hannah could see that Julius took pride in his work and his kitchen.

"Hello Julius, what are you cooking?"

"Oh, I decided to fix a little something for lunch. You hungry?"

Maybe if I keep her in here for a while," he thought, "she'll stop wandering around the house. Then I can get something done, including dinner for this evening.

"I'm starved, was Hannah's response."

"Well, have a seat."

Hannah sat down on a stool at the bar that was part of an island that doubled as a prepping station in the center of the kitchen. Julius had placed various vegetables in the sink.

"Is this part of what you're making?" Hannah asked, trying to make conversation.

"No that's part of dinner. How do you like it here, Hannah?

"It has taken some getting used to, but I'm adapting. The quiet doesn't bother me because I'm from the country, so I'm used to that. The size of this house well..., that's something else altogether. How long have you been here, Julius?"

"Oh, about some forty odd years."

"So, you've known Naboth for some time?"

"Yes, I have."

Hannah decided not to play any more games with Julius. At the risk of being rejected, she decided to reach out to him.

"Julius, I don't mean Naboth any harm. I hope you realize that."

Hannah's honest declaration took Julius by surprise, rendering him speechless. He didn't know how to respond. Becoming increasingly uncomfortable, he was glad when she continued talking.

"I mean that, Julius. Naboth brought me here totally on his own, Hannah said, going on to explain their chance meeting."

"I'm very protective of him, you know," Julius offered.

"Do tell," Hannah Thought.

Julius continued, "He's so vulnerable since his sister's death. I'm not going to allow anyone to take advantage of him. Anyway, I promised his sister Julia that I'd take care of him, and I'm a man who keeps his promises."

"I know, Julius. I promise you I won't take advantage. So, can we call a truce now?"

"Yea, I guess so." After the truce was called, the curt edginess between them was eased. Hannah hadn't realized how much she had missed the comfort of simple chitchat. She'd viewed her relationship with Naboth purely business. She was more focused and intent on impressing him with her education and expertise, she made it a point not to get into personal conversations with him. Although...they did have their moments, like the time in the garden. Sometimes they might broach a personal conversation in the middle of talking business...yet she still felt uncomfortable, finding it hard to initiate idle banter into their conversations.

Sitting in the kitchen with Julius in the relaxed leisurely atmosphere, Hannah unleashed. She told Julius about Hadaran, Granmama, Uncle Ivey and the myriad of hometown folks she grew up with. Describing them in such comical detail, she had Julius laughing himself to tears.

"Boy, when you get to talking, you're like a freight train late for a St. Louis run!" Julius quipped.

Hannah looked at Julius with a quizzical look on her face. Her forehead wrinkled up. As he looked at her, she said...

"A St. Louis what?" Realizing she didn't understand the analogy, they both fell into uproarious laughter. Hannah hadn't felt so free and easy in a while. What with school, coupled with the stress of finding employment, the two combined had taken their toll on Hannah's sense of humor. She didn't think she had any humor left, much less sense. Yes, it felt good to laugh again.

"Julius, Hannah said, changing the subject."

"Yes, Hannah."

"Do you know anything about the people in the portraits in the hall?"

"Yes, Mr. Vanderhoten started to research his family tree as a hobby not long after Julia died. I suppose it was sort of therapeutic for him.

Along the way he collected photographs and had some of them redone in oil, so he could build a gallery of sorts," Julius chuckled. "Naboth has found some interesting characters along the way, but…"

"But what, Julius?"

"Mr. Vanderhoten has shared with me just about everything he's ever found out about his family. He's kept me abreast of his progress, people, and places, recently, suddenly, Hannah, he's gotten really secretive."

"About what?"

"That's just it. I don't know, at least I don't know why he stopped sharing with me. The last time he said anything about his searching he was all worked up, real excited. He told me he had found a relative he hadn't known about. Something about a cousin, his great grandfather's brother's son, or something like that. He said he found some important information, but he's been quiet ever since. The next thing I knew, he hired that detective. He hasn't mentioned anything to me since."

"The day I first arrived, when I was trying to find the restroom, I saw him with a man, Hannah injected. Was that him?"

Julius looked at Hannah out of the corner of his eye, as Hannah said,

"No, Julius, really I got lost. I wasn't spying honest. He was a weird looking outfit." Hannah smiled as she used one of Granmama's colloquialisms, 'outfit.' That was granmama's way of describing a person who seemed strange to her. Anyway, she went on, Naboth didn't bother to introduce us. Wow! This is mysterious."

"Don't you go getting any ideas, Hannah. Stay out of Mr. Vanderhoten's business."

"Now, now, Julius what makes you think…?

"I'm just reading your expression, Hannah."

"Intriguing isn't it? Hannah's imaginings were running away. All the pieces were in place as if she were living a novel she'd read as a teen. Naboth the rich eccentric, Julius the butler, the detective, the mansion and the mysterious missing relative. Hannah's imagination took flight.

"Hannah!" came Julius' booming voice snapping Hannah back to reality.

"Ok, ok, I heard you. I promise I'll stay out of it, but you have to admit Julius doesn't it pique your curiosity, even a little?"

"Yes, but I trust Mr. Vanderhoten. In time, his time, he'll let me in. Until then, you and I agree to respect his privacy. Deal?"

Hannah remained silent, still in the "novel" of imagination.

"Deal?" Julius repeated.

"Deal," Hannah reluctantly replied.

Chapter Ten

"Hello Julius!"

"Mr. Vanderhoten, Sir."

"How's everything going? Is Hannah doing well?"

"Yes, Sir, everything is fine. She took a break, had a bite to eat, and has since returned to the library. I believe she's anticipating your return. Her assignment is pretty much complete, and she is anxious to show it to you. Those are her words, Sir."

"Very well, Julius. I have one more appointment. Then I will be returning home and should arrive at about six or seven at the latest. See you then, Julius."

"Yes Sir, good-bye."

Julius had never seen Naboth make so much fuss over anyone except for Julia. "God, I hope Hannah is sincere, he thought. The last thing Naboth needs is another encounter with disappointment and grief.

This past year has been hard on him, and it's evident in his behavior sometimes. "I suppose I shouldn't be so hard on Hannah. After all, I began my employ under great scrutiny."

Julius began to stare at the kitchen eyes roaming, looking at nothing in particular. Mesmerized by the ticking movement of the clock's second hand "Julius remarked to himself, "I've never noticed how loud that thing sounds."

Yes, Julia gave me one hell of a time when I first arrived. She thought Naboth had lost his mind and she let Naboth know, in no uncertain terms.

Hannah becoming discontented being alone, headed back to the kitchen, calling out to Julius as she entered.

"Julius!" Julius jumped startled by the sound of Hannah's voice. Hannah chuckled, seeing Julius jump.

"I'm sorry, did I scare you? I just wanted to know had you heard from Naboth yet?"

"No, and yes, he said he'd be home around six or seven."

"I'm sorry Julius, I didn't mean to startle you. I thought I would come back for a visit. Actually, I didn't want to be alone.

"It's ok Hannah. I suppose I was in some pretty deep thought. You caught me off guard."

Julius' thoughts continued drifting, like the ebbing and flowing of the tides, taking him further and further back to that fateful day in South Carolina.

Hannah was puzzled by Julius' peculiar behavior he was totally unaware of her presence.

"Julius," Hannah ventured, softly speaking, cautious.

"You know," Julius said, speaking hypnotically. Had it not been for the fortunate hand of God through Naboth, I'd either be dead or in prison on some chain-gang for the rest of my life. More than likely, the latter."

Hannah sat down, spellbound by his words.

Julius could feel his body tense as he remembered Luther Runnels. He had made it up in his mind, He wasn't going to allow him to disrespect his mama anymore. The next time Luther did... Julius shivered, frowning at the thought.

"I had to protect my mama Hannah," he turned to her. "I was all she had. On this particular day it seemed like something snapped inside of me." It didn't happen all at once, Julius, paused, deep in thought. but the results of years of overt, methodical attack of his manhood.

"Every time this man Luther would come around," he spoke to Hannah again. You see he came to collect the weeks take from share croppin'. My daddy wasn't around. And Luther you see, he'd get all up, on my mama. Looking at her in this lustful way he had. Only this time he touched her. I couldn't take it anymore. I remember my mama screaming, "Julius, don't! Boy, don't."

"But it was too late."

"What did you do Julius," Hannah said, intensely.

"I hit Luther, sent him reeling. The look on my face must have sent him a clear message. that and utter shock, when he realized he wasn't dealing with a child anymore.

Julius chuckled, remembering the look on Luther's face. "That hit I gave him, was a jolt of reality, it wasn't a little boy he was dealing with; That's how much attention Luther hadn't paid to me over the years. It was as if I didn't exist"

"What did Luther do," Hannah's asked with growing excitement.

"He said to me, do you know what you did Boy?" he kept saying, do you know what you did? You hit a white man, I'm going to get the sheriff, and have you arrested.

He never made it back. Meanwhile, mama started packing my clothes, preparing to get me out of town. Before she could finalize everything, the Sheriff showed up and arrested me for murdering Luther."

Hannah's mouth fell open, stunned, staring at Julius.

"To this day, Luther's death is still a mystery. Some say it was Red Neck Pete, his assistant of sorts. He rode around with Luther on collection days', something like a bodyguard. No one had seen hide nor hair of Pete, after that either. We all figured Luther told him what had happened, and Pete took advantage of the situation to rob Luther and hang his murder on me. Pete was always complaining about Luther's treating him no more than a "step above the Nigra's."

"One thing I learned that day Hannah, among others, you don't have to die to know what death is like, just come close."

"What do you mean Julius?"

"Well, it's like one's soul begins to separate itself from everything that connects it to life. Then you feel helpless, so helpless, all traces of hope are gone. And hope is the strength of a man Hannah. When a man is staring death in the face with no hope, he's left in utter darkness and begins to accept death as imminent. Yet he still breathes, and his heart continues to beat. Tears filled Julius eyes as he recalled the faces of the men screaming out for his blood. "The fear, it was overwhelming; I wouldn't wish it on my worst enemy Hannah."

"I...I...don't know what to say, Julius."

"Well anyway," he said, as he quickly wiped his eyes with the back of his hand, feeling a little embarrassed and vulnerable with Hannah, but continued.

Then in walks Naboth and a friend of his. Apparently, the sheriff didn't believe I was guilty. But he had to save face with the town folk. Decided he could blame some fancy pant, Jew lawyer from up North, then risk offending the people of his town. The Sheriff's plan was for Naboth to take the brunt of the repercussions since he was from out of town and would be leaving." Recalling what happened after that, brought a semi-cheerful smile to Julius' face.

"He listened to me; I'll never forget." Not only did he listen, he believed me."

He said. "We have to get you out of here."

"I didn't realize he meant that literally. Neither did I know until later what had taken place, including paying off the sheriff." "You see, Naboth had gone to see my mother, reassuring her of my safety and informing her he would be taking me away. He must have known some pretty influential people. Before I could say, 'what's going on,' I was being led from the jail into the back of a wagon, after riding for what seemed an eternity, we finally stopped." "I still believed I was being carried to my death. We finally stopped, when the tarp was removed, there stood Naboth and a group of his friends."

"Naboth explained to me his plan: I had to leave South Carolina right then and there, never to return. He'd promised Mama he would take care of me. I suppose it was at that moment he decided to take me home with him. I've been here ever since, thankful for what he'd done."

"Well, Julius, Hannah said." If I didn't understand before, I realize now, why you're so protective of Naboth."

"I suppose I kind of fell into the role of being his right-hand man, what some would call a butler. Partly from loyalty, partly from wanting to show Naboth how grateful I was. Although in his defense, I must say, Naboth has never made me feel as if I owed him anything. Nevertheless, as a man of principle, I believe in paying my way. That's how my mama raised me."

Hannah thoughtfully, "I know what you mean. Granmama taught me the same thing."

Julius nodded in agreement. "Eventually, Naboth and I found a comfortable rhythm to our relationship, and we've maintained it. Over the years, we've gleaned knowledge from one another. We've both realized our experiences in life, were not as distant as we thought. The more we shared, the more the cultural differences decreased, and our friendship increased."

"And Julia, how did she respond, Hannah asked hesitantly, not wanting to pry too much?

"I suppose Julia had a right to be suspicious, wondering whether I did or did not commit murder. But as years go by time has a way of curing things. We too found our rhythm and formed a natural bond that lasted until her death. I miss her as much as Naboth does, if not more. I spent a lot of time with her during her illness. Julia opened to me, places in her heart not many were allowed to enter. Not even her husband. I will take what she revealed to my grave."

Hannah sighed a deep sigh, staring at Julius. A moment of silence drifted between them. The emotional quandary that followed had Julius wondering why he felt safe, sharing the most significant part of his life with a total stranger. Meanwhile, Hannah contemplated her own mortality and purpose.

Chapter Eleven

The meeting with Scott had gone well. He was making progress. But Naboth was anxious to get home. "Joseph, take me to the heliport."

"Yes, Sir," Joseph said, leading Naboth towards the car and opening the door.

. . . .

Flying into the estate took Naboth over the major portions of the vineyard. As they flew over the buildings that housed the wine vats and the caretaker's cottage, Naboth couldn't help but contemplate the enormity of his success in life.

"What does it all mean? Has it been worth it? More importantly, to whom will it all be left? Wise King Solomon once said, 'material wealth is all vanity and vexation of a man's spirit," Naboth thought, releasing a deep sigh.

"Why didn't I ever marry," Naboth asked, continuing with his reflections. "I suppose it's too late now. Who would want an old man, like me? I don't have the audacity to do what some of my peers have done, marry someone ten to fifteen years younger. My friend Samuel even had the nerve to have another child at his age. My God, what was he thinking! Naboth chuckled to himself. "Although, he mused, it would be a way to procure an heir, h-m-m-m."

His reflections took him into areas of thinking he'd rather not go, including regrets. "My one regret is not having companionship at this time of my life. Someone to share my interests, a-n-d yes, my bed. This old coot could use some warming up now and then," Naboth smiled at the thought.

"Yes," he pondered, "Hannah's arrival was right on time, her youthful exuberance and intelligence, has infused a long-needed charge and change in the atmosphere of the mansion.

For the first time since his sister's death, he felt good about going home. He couldn't wait to see Hannah and hear her thoughts and suggestions.

. . . .

Sarah had never seen Naboth so eager to leave. Usually, he stayed long after everyone else had gone for the day, sometimes long into the night. The only time he had ever left early was during Julia's illness, to be with her. Before he would work such long hours, she became worried and concerned for his health.

"So, Sarah," she said aloud, "why are you concerned about his leaving early?" Isn't it a good thing or not?" Is it because he's being so elusive," He surely isn't my usual Naboth, she surmised?

"My Naboth?" she thought, laughing nervously.

Sarah, as a means of distraction, began to straighten things on an otherwise neat and orderly desk. Slowly she turned deep in thought and walked over to the window, staring out at the sunset. She'd always loved this office. The view was spectacular, and she often came in just to sit and reflect after Naboth had left for the day.

"He doesn't even know I exist except inside his world of business. He and I created a companionship through business and that's where it seems to have remained.

Sarah's pensive mood began to raise her worst fear. A developing premonition that someone would see past her superficial façade and discover the true feelings of her heart, to which she dared not give utterance to.

Since Julia's death, Sarah had spoken of her feelings to no one, but God. Julia had encouraged her to tell Naboth how she felt, but fear of rejection kept her quietly smoldering. Instead, she used small talk, false laughter, and everyday office routine to smother embers that would otherwise flare-up to engulf her. Content to admire and love him from a distance. Remaining his loyal friend and confidante.

"Although lately, she murmured, for the first time, I'm beginning to question our relationship.

"You're sounding bitter Sarah," she chastened herself.

"Sarah," Came the voice over the intercom, jolting her back from her pensive mood.

Rushing to Naboth's desk, she snapped. "Yes, Rachel. How many times have I told you not to use the intercom?"

"I...I...I'm sorry her assistant answered meekly.

Sarah felt bad for taking her personal feelings out on the poor girl. She had nothing to do with her emotional state of mind.

"It's ok Rachel, what can I do for you?"

Still apologizing, grating Sarah's already shattered nerve, Rachel said, "I'm sorry. You have a call from Roland Anderson."

"Thank you. I'll take it in here," Sarah sighed heavily, taking a deep breath while thinking, "Now, what does he want?"

Sarah was still in shock. It was just several weeks ago Roland had approached her regarding collaborating with him against Naboth.

How dare he even began to believe in his wildest imaginings that I would go along with him, Sarah thought. What bothers me even more is I haven't told Naboth. I really shouldn't keep something this crucial from him, yet…I have.

Contemplating her actions, Sarah thought, it's not that I don't want to tell him. It's just that we haven't had the time for a decent conversation as of late. It's been more of a coming and going relationship between us. I must schedule us to have lunch or dinner and warn him about Roland.

Sarah picked up the phone and said, "Roland, what can I do for you?"

Roland asked, "Is Naboth around?"

"No, Sarah replied, he left early not saying where he was going."

"Ok, thanks Sarah."

She's lying, Roland thought, as he hung up the phone. Naboth never leaves without letting her know his every move. I wonder, did she tell him about my approaching her? Damn, that was a stupid move. I was sure she was ready, especially after being spurned by Naboth all these years."

My timing was impeccable, so I thought. She's a tough cookie to be in love with him all these years. I figured by now she'd be fed up enough to join forces. Naboth is either blind or just plain stupid. I can't figure which, maybe a little of both.

"Has she told him?" he asked himself again. If she had wouldn't he have said something by now, confronted me? Either he's a fool or has plans of his own. Nah-h-h, Naboth isn't that smart. If she hasn't told him, why? Maybe she's still considering. Perhaps there's a chance she'll come over to my side of things.

"I know what I'll do. I'll send Sylvia over to his house this weekend and see if she can dig up any information. Naboth seems to have a soft spot for her because she looks so much like her mother. But that's where the similarity ends, he said with a sarcastic laugh."

It was true. Sylvia, from all outward appearances, was her mother's twin. Same delicate features, beautiful auburn hair, small and petite. However, there was a side to Sylvia that even chilled Roland at times.

She had a cold, calculating way of looking at and through a person, especially when they had crossed her.

It wasn't that I hadn't loved Julia, he queried, pondering his feelings. Even now at times, I miss her like crazy. She'd had a way of keeping me grounded and sane but...but... the women. Even when they knew I was married. They kept pulling at me, wouldn't leave me alone. I couldn't resist. I loved the attention, and Julia, through no fault of her own, couldn't keep up.

Naboth didn't make it any better. We were constantly at each other's throat. We argued constantly regarding what he called my indiscretions. Poor Julia was caught in the middle. Naboth tried to blame me for her death. But he was just as much at fault. Causing her to feel as if she had to choose between the two of us.

"I loved you Julia, truly I did," Roland moaned out loud.

Roland swiveled around in his chair looking out the window. His eyes leaped from skyscraper to skyscraper until coming to rest on the bridge and the horizon beyond. "It would be so easy," he thought. It is a way out. I wouldn't have to feel this aching in my soul."

Julia, she knew how. She knew how to touch his soul, how to reach him.

Her love was like a surgeon's knife. There were times he would come home with his manhood wounded. She would take the knife of her love and ever so gently make an incision. cutting through the skin of his pride, past the layer of male ego, until the hurt was exposed. Then with tender, purposeful words, she would ever so gently massage the wound. Afterward, close it with fine intimate sutures. She never let on she knew what she had done. Leaving his manhood intact, *that*, was his Julia.

"Enough, Roland," he jerked, redirecting his thoughts. "Back to the business at hand."

Standing and stretching, with a sly gleam in his eye, Roland sat on the corner of his desk and reached for the phone.

"Yes, Mr. Anderson," his secretary answered.

"Get my daughter on the phone for me."

Chapter Twelve

Having made his arrival, Naboth was greeted at the door by Julius.

"Good evening, Sir."

"Good evening, Julius. How was your day?"

"Uneventful."

"Now Julius, after being here with Hannah all day, as well as being so protective of me not to mention this house. Unless you and Hannah kept your distance, your day had to be more than uneventful."

Julius had to laugh at Naboth's insight.

"Well all right, I admit we had quite a conversation today."

"Good. I hope it settled some of the questions you've had regarding her and Hannah, the same concerning you. You two had me worried for a while, not knowing how or if the two of you were going to come to terms. Remember how it was with you and Julia when you first arrived?"

"Do I, those were trying times indeed. But we finally settled our differences, becoming the best of friends, Julius ended with a sigh.

"She loved you Julius. I expect no less between you and Hannah."

"Yes, Sir."

"Speaking of friends, where is Hannah?"

"She's preparing for dinner. I expect her at any moment. Would you like to freshen up before dinner, Sir?"

"How much time do I have?"

"About forty-five minutes to an hour."

"I think I'll go up and do just that, Julius. Tell Hannah I'll see her at dinner."

After freshening up, Hannah headed out of her room toward the stairs. Still getting used to her surroundings, she looked up at the ceiling and the walls in the hall admiring the intricate detail feeling like royalty as she made her way down the marble staircase. As she reached the main hall, she decided to go looking for Julius. Her search ended in the kitchen, finding him looming over the stove, stirring a pot of something that smelled delicious.

"Hi, Julius, what are you cooking?"

"How about letting it be a surprise?"

"Ok. Naboth home yet?"

"Yes. He said to tell you he'd join you at dinner."

"Julius?"

"Yes."

"Thanks for today. I hope we can be friends. I'm beginning to feel more comfortable about being here. I don't know, perhaps this is where I'm supposed to be, you know?"

"Even the portraits of Naboth's family lining the hall, when I look at them, I don't know, I feel somehow connected. I sound crazy, don't I?"

"No, not completely, Julius replied.

"Hannah laughed, "Not completely? What, just half?"

"No, that's not what I mean. It's just that Naboth has a way of making a person feel completely welcomed, not a stranger. He just has that way about him."

"I understand what you're saying. I don't think it's anything, probably because one of the women in a portrait reminded me of my great grandmamma, Julia. Great granmama' daddy was white, and her mama, a slave. I did some research on our family for a high school history project, it was interesting. I love history; it intrigues me. Sometimes it's kind of romantic."

"It depends on what you mean by "romantic." I can't think of anything romantic about my history. As a matter of fact, there are some parts I'd rather forget altogether."

"Ah-h-h, come on, Julius. You mean to tell me there isn't some lost love somewhere in your past that's worth remembering?"

Julius smiled as Bella slipped into and through his mind.

"Uh-huh. Look at you," Hannah joked. "Tell me, who is she?"

"I'll never tell. I'll take this one to my grave, young lady."

"But, Julius, aren't you the least bit curious or interested in where you came from, where your people came from?"

"I suppose things were so hard when I was growing up, especially after my dad died. When I left South Carolina, I left that part of my life behind except for my mama. I 'd rather let sleeping dogs lie."

"You've experienced a lot of hurt; haven't you, Julius?"

"No more than most folks of my generation who grew up in the South. Since then, I've learned a lot. I've learned to forgive and let go. I know what the experts say. I read a little too, you know."

"Ok, Julius, ok."

As Naboth descended the stairs, he was drawn to the echoing voices coming from the kitchen, "Am I interrupting, or can I get in on this conversation?" he said, coming through the kitchen door.

"Hi, Naboth, come on and join in," Hannah responded in between gulps of laughter. We were just discussing some of life's challenges and how to meet them according to Julius."

"Don't let Julius fool you, Naboth said firmly. Here stands before you a very wise and extremely intelligent man. I have complete confidence in his counsel."

Hannah smiled as she watched Julius blush with embarrassment from the compliment.

"Hannah, would you like to take a walk before dinner?" Naboth asked.

"Sure, I'd love to."

Chapter Thirteen

As Hannah and Naboth casually strolled through the garden, no words passed between them. What could have been an uneasy silence was pacified by mutual respect for each other's reflections.

The sun was just beginning to set behind the rise of the knoll, painting the sky a brilliant red orange reminding Hannah of the drawings she made as a child. A scraggly brown hill with a half sun painted yellow and half of the sky blue. The half closer to the sun red and orange. On the hill were flowers interspersed with lollipop shaped trees here and there; a child's perfect world.

As they mounted the crest of the knoll, Naboth spoke.

"Let's rest here for a moment Hannah. This was my sister's favorite spot. This is an original hill, or maybe I should say a mound of sorts. I was going to level it to make more space for planting. I came out here one day and realized that one could see both the vineyard and Julia's garden from up here. As you can see, visionary prowess paid off. The view is stunning. Julia would come here and sit for hours."

"It's Beautiful," Hannah said.

"So, Hannah, did you have a good day? I see you, and Julius found a way to break the ice between you. I'm pleased."

"We did lock horns initially, didn't we?"

"Yes, but two intelligent people like yourselves could not stay that way long, it would have been beneath you."

"How would you know that Naboth? I mean, you just seem to have an eye for seeing who people are beneath the surface."

"I'm not always right, Hannah."

"But... why me, Naboth?"

"And you asked that question again because, Naboth inquired with raised eyebrows, staring at Hannah intently?

"Hannah, I answered your question with a question, because it's important for you to know why. Do you not deserve it?" Self-confidence and a sense of value and worth are one of the things I hope you accomplish while here. You are a very gifted and talented young woman."

"I've struggled for years, pretty much all my life Naboth, with feelings of inadequacy. I have this sick need to be validated. It's like I know what I know. I know I am capable. But sometimes I get this mental block of uncertainty." I continually question my decisions, second guessing myself. I'm unsure, unless someone else validates it. For someone else to say yes, you're right Hannah. That's bad, don't you think?"

"I'll ask you again, what do you think. Do you think it's bad?"

You see Hannah, as human beings we all have at one time or another the need for validation. Or, just simply if you will, encouragement from one another. What a pitiable world it would be if no one ever complimented, or as you say, validated another."

"But not all the time Naboth. I'm sick with needing validation," Hannah said with a nervous chuckle.

Naboth smiled, "You're young, Hannah, not long out of school. You're just beginning to get your feet wet. Experiences good or bad is what develops confidence."

"I can see good experiences doing that, but how does a bad experience develop confidence?"

"You'll understand one day, Hannah. Bad experiences have a way of stretching us, pulling us into places we would not dare go. We take steps with the good, stretch with the bad, and between the two, we grow and mature."

Hannah smiled at Naboth. She felt truly safe, welcomed. Reassured that it was ok for her to be here with Naboth. Peace saturated her flowing like a cool meandering stream into her heart, creating a reservoir of calming assurance deep within. It was a place she knew she'd be able to draw from when needed.

"Shall we go to dinner, My Lady," Naboth playfully joked with Hannah, as he extended his arm to her. They walked back to the house, laughing and talking like old friends.

Just as Julius was on his way to find Hannah and Naboth to announce dinner, they came through the door, followed by a delightful floral scent wafting in from the garden. The 'scent mingled with the new-found camaraderie and laughter between Naboth and Hannah.

Julius couldn't help but smile as he reminisced. "It's been a long time since we've had that kind of laughter in this house, he thought. It feels good."

God, I hate to ruin his evening. But Sylvia called. I've got to warn him of her arrival this weekend.

"I wonder what she really wants. Whatever it is, you can bet her father is either behind it, in on it, or both. Those two are like two peas in a pod. I'll wait until Hannah is safely out of hearing range, then I'll inform him."

. . . .

"Julius, dinner was absolutely wonderful. You outdid yourself Julius, as usual," Naboth said.

"Yes, it was, Julius," Hannah, chimed in. "I loved it."

"Thank you. You are both too kind."

Hannah and Naboth laughed at Julius's efforts at modesty.

"All right that's enough from you two," Julius chuckled.

Naboth gave Hannah a wink as they continued to tease Julius.

"Are you ready to show me your presentation, Hannah?" Naboth asked, after catching Julius' signal of needing to talk to him in private.

"Yes, it's up in my room, I'll run get it," Hannah answered, rising to leave.

"Very well, I'll meet you in the library."

As Hannah was leaving the room, she overheard Julius mention to Naboth he had a phone call while he and Hannah were in the garden.

"This isn't good, Julius. Did Sylvia say why she wanted to come for a visit?"

"No, she didn't, just that she was coming. You know how she feels about me. She wouldn't have told me anyway."

"I'm not ready to reveal Hannah to Sylvia just yet, Julius. I need more time. Roland has been a bit edgy lately. He's up to something; I just know it. "He's the one who interviewed Hannah for the job, then turned her down."

"I met, or should I say literally ran into Hannah down in the lobby after her interview. It was not a pretty sight. She was very upset, to the point of tears. I have no idea what he said to her. Anyway, I offered her a ride and... Well, you know the rest. Damn them, I wanted to win Hannah's trust. It's important she trusts me."

"Don't underestimate Hannah, Julius said reassuringly." "She just said to me earlier today that she feels like she belongs here. That somehow this is where she's supposed to be."

"She said that?"

"Yes, Sir, she did."

"Then Julius, it is even more pertinent that we protect her at this time. I can't let them know about her presence just yet."

"Didn't you discuss with her several weeks ago about taking a business trip regarding the project she's working on?

"You knew about that?"

"Hannah told me about it during one of our talks, Julius responded sheepishly. So why can't she go this weekend," he offered.

"Julius, you're brilliant! After we go over her presentation, I'll suggest she prepare to go this weekend. What I've seen so far is excellent. I think she's ready anyway. I was just waiting for her to feel comfortable and confident about her task."

"Then that's your answer, it shouldn't raise any suspicion on her part."

"I hope I'm making the right decision, Julius. It has to be."

As Hannah entered the library, she couldn't help but notice the strange look on Naboth and Julius' faces not to mention the sudden silence that greeted her. "I suppose they can have secrets between them," she concluded. "They've known each other a long time. They would naturally share some secrets between themselves."

Hannah knew she was rationalizing to make up for the slight angst she felt, pushing aside the uneasy feeling. Her mood quickly changed as she thought about her presentation. I'm finally getting the opportunity to impress Naboth with my work. Hannah couldn't help but smile.

Even though Hannah believed she gave an excellent, thorough presentation, she was still shocked at the suddenness of Naboth's decision.

"Why don't you go this weekend," he said.

"Are you serious?" Hannah exclaimed.

"Were you not the one who said that your figures and analysis couldn't be completed unless you visited the actual sites? Among the other things you've been learning, I've given you ample enough time. Don't you think it's time, Hannah?"

Hannah sat, stunned.

"What's wrong Hannah?" Naboth pressed.

Hannah barely heard Naboth's question.

Answering, "Nothing I…I… guess. I thought I would have more time to get used to the idea, but if you think I can handle it, ok, I suppose."

"Hannah, listen to me." Naboth felt deceitful, although he truly knew Hannah was ready. It was time to put her talents to use. Hannah's going wasn't what Naboth questioned. The reason behind, the suddenness of her going, brought him pangs of guilt.

"You can do this my dear, you're ready. You've been in school for the past eight years studying. Now it's time for you to apply all that knowledge you've acquired. Do you honestly believe I would send you if I were not totally confident in your ability? I've been training you for several weeks, a little over a month for this, you've learned quickly. It's time."

"No, I don't suppose you would, Naboth. This is it isn't it? Either I want to do this, or I don't. I've been complaining about not being recognized and not being able to use my skills. Look at me, trying to find an excuse for not doing it. Yes, you're right," she resolved. "I'll prepare to leave. When, Naboth?"

"How about Friday? That way you'll have the weekend to rest up, play the tourist, relax then get a fresh start at your first site on Monday morning. How's that?"

"Good, it's good Naboth." Hannah agreed outwardly, but inwardly, she toiled with and questioned the feeling of being rushed."

Her forehead wrinkled in thought. Inside her, there was also a rush of excitement brewing, one she could hardly contain. She had finally become a woman of purpose, in total charge of her first assignment.

Chapter Fourteen

Hannah had an early flight. Rising early and showering, she felt a quiver of exhilaration pulsate through her. Not so much from the shower, as from the mounting excitement over what lay ahead.

Joseph was waiting for her as she came out the door. Having already loaded her luggage, he helped her into the car. Hannah's exuberance blinded her to Joseph's anxiousness to get her into the car and be off. Unknown to her, he had been informed of an approaching car. Possibly Sylvia arriving early for which Mr. Vanderhoten had planned. Joseph couldn't help but grin as he thought what a wise man Mr. Vanderhoten was. Yes, a wise man indeed.

Perusing through her notes, Hannah looked up just as they were passing another limo headed in the direction of the mansion. Straining to peer through the tinted windows of the limo, she said aloud, "Who could that be?"

"You say something, Mam?"

"No, Joseph, just wondering who's headed to the house this early in the morning. Maybe it's that detective Naboth hired," she mumbled. Accepting the inference, she returned to reading her notes.

Sylvia turned her head, trying to look behind her, while thinking, "That was Uncle Naboth's driver. I hope Uncle hasn't left. Even if I did say I wouldn't be arriving until Saturday morning.... but what's the fun of arriving on the day I told him, I can't find out anything that way. It's the element of surprise that will get them every time, she remarked to herself. If there's anything going on, this is the way to find out. However, I'm just about fed up with Father using me for his dirty work. I should start charging him.

What am I supposed to be looking for anyway? What does father think I'll find? 'Whatever looks suspicious,' he'd said. Whatever that means," she gushed aloud in exasperation.

• • • •

Joseph had phoned the mansion, informing Naboth of what he and Julius had predicted. Sylvia's early arrival. Naboth was glad they decided Hannah would take an early flight.

"I hate this," he thought. "I really don't like being misleading. But timing is everything. It's not advantageous to reveal Hannah just yet.

"I wonder what Sylvia wants?"

Sylvia rolled down the limo window, allowing the morning sun to warm her face while she feasted her eyes upon the beauty of the vineyard as they passed by.

"So much land," she thought. "Perhaps, if I play my cards right, it will be mine someday. If not all at least a portion of it. Daddy seems to think I'm Uncle Naboth's favorite. The only competition I would have is David. Uncle Naboth can't stand Saul. He places Saul in the same category as Father. M-mph, half the time I can't stand Saul. Nevertheless, if I am Uncles favorite, I can't do anything to jeopardize my standing with him. I will not allow Father to push this spying thing too far."

Sylvia leaned back. The breeze coming in through the open window beckoned the free spirit part of her. For the moment she gave permission for the stuffy, pompous Sylvia to retreat as her liberated self, luxuriated in the picture-perfect scenery. Sun glistening off emerald green leaves of the grapevines as every now and then a cluster of purple grapes were made visible through the jungle of leaves, by the warm summer breeze.

Sylvia was her father's eldest, followed by the two boys. She was jealous of her brothers at first. But her mother had a way of making her feel special as her only daughter.

A smile played at her lips as the memory of her mother settled in. The memory lovingly embracing her thoughts. "Mother was so sweet and gentle, never raising her voice. "Because she didn't have to, she found herself saying out loud." We all held her in high regard, respecting her completely, me Saul and David."

"Now Father, well, their relationship with him was the direct opposite. How those two got together is beyond me, she pondered. However, father is a charmer. I can see why mother was smitten by him.

"We're here Miss," came the suddenness of the driver's voice, jolting Sylvia back to the present.

"We're here, Miss," he repeated as they came to a stop.

"Yes, thank you," Sylvia said, getting out of the car. She hesitated, stood for a moment looking up at the mansion, while the driver retrieved her bags.

It was beautiful. Perhaps opulent in its own way, yet it still embraced all visitors with a feeling of hearth and home. It was her mother who created the warm, inviting atmosphere. Her Mother's obvious skills expressed through her choices of furnishings and decorations.

"And, oh the garden!" she thought, remembering made her smile.

How she loved to play among the rows of manicured hedges, pretending that the roses, peonies, daffodils and the other flowers and plants were part of her magic fairytale kingdom.

Nor could she forget the special times alone with her mother, away from her brothers and father. Her mother fondly referred to it as their "girl time." They would walk together hand in hand, up to the knoll that overlooked the vineyard and garden. They'd spent a lot of time there just before her mother's death. Perhaps I'll visit, while I'm here," she thought, "then again," she said in a melancholy whisper, "perhaps not."

Chapter Fifteen

Sylvia could have walked in without knocking, for the most part, it was home. But her mother's lessons in etiquette coupled with her natural penchant towards proper social conduct, persuaded her to ring the doorbell instead.

Julius answered the door.

"Hi, Julius."

"Good morning, Miss Sylvia."

"Oh Julius, not so formal, please. It's Sylvia, these *are* the nineties."

"Yes, Mam."

Naboth heard the doorbell and headed to the foyer to greet his niece.

"Sylvia, my dear!"

"Uncle Naboth, how are you? It's so good to see you."

"It's good to see you as well. We weren't expecting you until tomorrow."

"I know, but I forgot a prior engagement. So, I decided to come today and leave tomorrow morning. I hope I didn't inconvenience you."

"No, no not to worry. How are your brothers?"

"David is doing very well. He's still at Harvard, and hopefully, he will graduate soon with a degree in law.

"And Saul?"

"Well..., you know, he's still being Saul."

"Yes, yes indeed, but we'll keep hoping. And your father, Naboth asked?"

"He's fine as well. Now that all the pleasantries are out of the way, tell me, how are you doing, Uncle? I mean really. I've been concerned about you. I realize mother's death must have been hard on you."

"Well, it has been a little over a year and a half. We all must move on. I would like to think that is what I am doing, moving on. Now, tell Uncle what you are doing here, really?"

Sylvia strained a laugh, "Why Uncle, to see about you of course."

Naboth couldn't help raising an eyebrow while hoping Sylvia hadn't noticed. Perhaps he should give her the benefit of a doubt.

"Well, well. He couldn't think of anything else to say."

"I know you're surprised, but it's true, nevertheless. Of course, father asked me to come also."

Naboth couldn't believe she admitted to her father's being in on her visit.

"Now tell me," he said, as they sat down together in the great room with Julius serving tea. "When is your wedding? When are you and...?

"Nesbitt, Uncle."

"Yes, of course, Nesbitt? What kind of name is Nesbitt?"

"An old family name passed down from his father's side, Sylvia said proudly."

"Perhaps, that is something that should have been kept in the past."

"Ha! Ha! Ha!" Uncle, you are so right, they should have. I prefer to call him Nezz. It's a little better."

"And his last name?"

"Peterson."

"Nesbitt Peterson, m-m-m, quaint isn't it."

Sylvia laughed again, genuinely enjoying her Uncle's dry sense of humor. "Julius, you can go ahead and laugh too. I see the corner of your mouth turning up.

Julius hurriedly exited the room. When he was out of earshot, he laughed so hard, tears began to stream down his face. "Nesbitt," he thought. With a name like that he must have fought all through school."

"I see Julius is still hanging on," Sylvia surmised while wondering what kind of provision her Uncle had made for him and how much of the estate he would inherit. Other than her younger brother, Julius may also be a cause for concern. Her Uncle and Julius were close. She'd learned that the hard way.

Shortly after her mother's death, she'd made the mistake of suggesting it was time to let Julius go. She had been trying to clean up that fiasco ever since. She had smiled and sucked up so much that she made herself sick. However, what she stood to inherit was worth all the sucking up she had to do.

"So, Uncle, what else is new? Are you still doing the family tree thing?"

Knowing Sylvia was not genuinely interested, Naboth decided to go along with the charade. She had made it perfectly clear to him the nonimportance of looking into one's past. "The future is what's important," she'd said. "So much to look forward to, the operative word here, Uncle, being forward."

"Yes, I'm still plugging along. Although I have found some very interesting information about our family, I can't wait to complete my research. And once I do, I plan to share it with all of you."

"Yes... sure... can't wait," Sylvia said, with barely veiled sarcasm.

"Uncle, I'm going up to my room to freshen up and rest a bit before lunch. I had such an early start this morning I could use a nap."

"Yes, yes, of course, My Dear, you go right ahead. It'll give me some time to work on a few things and make some phone calls."

"My same room as usual, right?"

"Why...uh, yes," Naboth said hesitatingly while thinking, "Oh, my God, which room did Hannah occupy? I don't know."

Unknown to Naboth, Julius had locked the door of the adjoining bathroom between Hannah's room and the one Sylvia would occupy.

"Damn," Julius muttered aloud, "I forgot to check the bathroom. I locked the door but forgot to check the bathroom. Stupid. I'd better warn Naboth in case some of Hannah's toiletries were left behind." Julius hurried to tell Naboth.

"Thanks, Julius, don't worry about moving it now. If there were anything; to remove it now would promote more suspicion. I'll think of something."

"Yes Sir, I'm sorry."

"No apology necessary, Julius. I'm sorry I had to drag you into this whole mess."

"Well, Sir, if you don't mind my saying, it's kind of fun outwitting Miss Sylvia. I'm actually enjoying it."

"I really hadn't thought of it that way. But when you look at the overall picture, it is kind of comical, isn't it?"

As Sylvia topped the stairs, she recalled the times she and her brothers played tag and hide n' seek, up and down the second-floor hall. Running in and out of the many rooms. Then there were those serendipitous moments when their mother would join in, making it even more fun.

Sylvia unpacked her overnight case, meticulously laying her dinner attire across a chaise that sat in the center of the room. She walked across the bedroom, heading to the bathroom, surveying the room as she went.

While looking in the bathroom mirror, she noticed an array of bath products along the back of the tub, behind her. "Bath oil, bubble bath?" She asked herself.

Turning, she walked over to the tub and said in a tone of discovery, "M-m-m, and what do we have here, perhaps one of Father's, 'whatever looks suspicious?' Maybe daddy was right after all. Either Uncle has switched up on us, or there's been a woman in this house. The brands aren't bad either. She has expensive taste, whoever she is."

Sylvia turned slowly in a circle, surveying the room as she looked for more signs of the presence of a female. Finding nothing else, she postponed her curiosity by putting herself on notice to do some more snooping later. She was beginning to feel tired, having risen so early. Half stumbling to the bed, she laid down. Curled up into a ball, falling fast asleep.

. . . .

The echoes of laughter resounded through the mansion and up the stairs waking Sylvia. She got up, showered, dressed, and headed downstairs. Following the sounds of the continual laughter, she arrived in the great room, coming upon her Uncle and Julius.

Hey, you two, what's so funny? I heard the two of you all the way upstairs."

"Oh, it's nothing. It' a man's thing, kind of an inside joke. You wouldn't understand," Naboth offered.

"Also known as 'none of your business'," Sylvia said sarcastically.

"You said it, My Dear, not us. Did you sleep well"?

'Don't try to change the subject, Uncle. In answer to your question, as a matter of fact, I did. I didn't realize how tired I was. I was out as soon as my head hit the pillow. How long was I asleep? I hope I didn't miss lunch, Julius. I'm famished."

"No, Mam, I was just getting ready to serve," Julius said, excusing himself, to go and get lunch.

"Uncle, as I passed the library, I saw how neat it was. I don't think I've seen it so organized. Julius did an excellent job."

"I'm glad you like it, but it isn't Julius' work. I hired a young intern to come in and assist me. She did a wonderful job, didn't she? It took her a while, she had to spend several days. You must have seen some of her toiletries left on the tub upstairs. Julius was cleaning the other day and said some of her things were left in the bathroom. Surely you noticed?"

"Uh…well…uh…yes, but I thought never mind what I thought," Sylvia said.

"Yes dear?" Naboth said, looking down at his plate, thinking, "You could buy Sylvia with a nickel the look on her face is priceless." He kept his head down, stifling a smile and thought, "Julius was right. This is fun; however, it isn't over. She's going to drill me to find out the woman's identity. I hope my explanation was enough to sate her curiosity.

After lunch, Sylvia spent the rest of the afternoon in the garden and library. She couldn't bring herself to go up on the knoll, too many memories. Off and on throughout the day, she had casual conversations with her Uncle.

"There's nothing to be found here," she thought. "I don't know what Father is looking for. Whatever it is, he won't get the results he wanted I'm sure of it. Unless there's something to this intern, but I doubt it. Uncle's explanation sounds legitimate to me. The library was a mess, in fact, a disaster. I can't believe it's the same room. I've spent more time in there than I ever have. It felt comfortable and pleasant.

Dinner was just as uneventful Sylvia was so bored, she drank too much wine bordering idiocy.

Finally, she excused herself, "Uncle, I'm going to call it a night. I plan to leave early tomorrow morning. Nezz and I have a charity event to attend, and I want to get back early enough to do all the necessary female preparations. You know, hairdresser, a facial, I have several appointments."

"Yes, I understand dear. I remember your mother doing some of the same things. You go right ahead. I'm going to enjoy a gentlemen's cigar and turn in myself."

"Goodnight, Uncle."

"Goodnight, Sylvia."

"Mr. Vanderhoten, you have a phone call Sir," Julius said.

"Thanks, Julius, I'll take it in the library."

"Who could be calling this late," Sylvia wondered, the announcement pricking her curiosity. She decided to do some snooping before going up for the night. Pretending to go upstairs, Sylvia doubled back and tipped-toed her way down the hall to the library, unaware of the eyes that were watching her. Leaning against the side of the double doors that were partially closed; she quietly leaned over to sneak a quick peek to see where Naboth was. The only light in the room was a small desk lamp.

"What does she think she's doing?" Julius chuckled quietly, watching from across the hall in an adjacent room so as not to be seen.

Facing the door, Sylvia slowly inched her way until she came to the edge. Grabbing the doors' edge, she leaned into the room ever so slightly, straining to get into a position to listen. Having leaned in such an awkward position in heels, Sylvia suddenly lost her footing. She would have fallen headlong into the room had she not grabbed the door with her other hand. Quickly pulling herself up, she pressed hard against the door, seeking to lose herself in the darkness of the hall.

"Who's there?" Naboth called out.

"Hold on a minute," Naboth said to the caller.

Sylvia held her breath, hearing Naboth's steps getting closer and closer.

Naboth walked to the door and pushed it hard, slamming it shut, unaware of the fingers wrapped around its edge.

Sylvia let out a squeak, snatching her hand out of harm's way just in time then scurried down the hall to the safety of the stairs and eventually to her room. As she closed her door, she heard laughter.

Julius slid down the side of the wall to the floor. With both hands covering his mouth, muffling his hysterical laughter. Tears were streaming down his face, his body shaking mercilessly from having watched the scene unfold before him. He finally found the strength to pull himself together and hurried to the library to share with Naboth Sylvia's attempt at spying and eavesdropping.

Sylvia trying desperately to calm herself, leaned against her bedroom door. Her wobbly legs wouldn't allow her to take another step. She barely made it up the stairs. The last thing she wanted was her Uncle to catch her trying to eavesdrop on his conversation. All her plans would have gone up in smoke. Stumbling weak kneed to the bathroom she doused her face with cold water and decided to take a shower. Sylvia allowed the warm spray of the shower to relax her, still wondering who the caller could have been.

After her shower, Sylvia crawled into bed. She heard more laughter echoing through the hall and up the stairs." They're getting on my nerves with that incessant laughter," she said critically as she closed her eyes.

The next morning Sylvia met with her Uncle to have breakfast before her departure.

"Good morning, Sylvia," Naboth said.

"Good morning, Uncle Naboth."

Small talk was the order of the morning. Sylvia was dying to ask her Uncle about the phone call. But when he didn't offer, she concluded it would be best not to.

"Everything all right dear?" Naboth asked.

"Yes, Uncle. Thanks for having me over."

"You're quite welcome, Sylvia."

"I will always love this place. It holds such wonderful memories of mother and our growing-up years."

Naboth thought he heard a hint of sincerity in her voice until she said, "But, that's the past we must move on. Right?"

"If that's what you believe, Sylvia. Come I'll walk you to the car."

Naboth and Sylvia walked through the mansion from the garden room in a somewhat strained sort of quiet but not tense enough to be uncomfortable. It was as if they were both uncertain of what should be said, so neither one said nothing. They had exhausted all the usual pleasantries, and it was time to simply say good-bye.

Before getting into the car, Sylvia said, "I love you Uncle, even though you believe digging into the past is so important. Bye, love."

"Bye, Sylvia. "Watching the car until it was out of sight, Naboth felt a rush of anxiety regarding the destiny of his nephews and niece. He thought, I'm so grateful Julia is not here to see Saul. It would devastate her to see him in his condition. She had such high hopes for all her children. David nonetheless has been encouraging. He seems to be the most grounded of the three and most like his mother. Yes... Naboth decided, David gives me hope."

Chapter Sixteen

The trip had been productive more than Hannah had hoped for. She was pleased with what she had accomplished. When she spoke with Naboth, he seemed to agree with her findings. What was puzzling to her is that he couldn't or wouldn't tell her who this mysterious Mr. Anderson was. His response was guarded, telling her to not make any decision until meeting with him, when she returned.

"Anyway," she sighed, "whoever he is, he doesn't know a thing about management. Especially when it comes to employer-employee relationships, it was as if his decisions were intentional. As if he wanted the businesses to fail. Yes, she decided, it was intentional. But why? His decisions were deliberate, deliberate enough to produce failure.

The general managers were in a quandary. They never knew from one day or week to the next what would transpire. There was growing hostility and distrust among the employees toward upper management. They were glad to finally have someone from corporate to visit and hopefully bring meaningful solutions to their growing concerns.

She also found out they were a subsidiary company. So, who was the main corporation behind them? Naboth hadn't shared that bit of information with her. She couldn't believe she missed it. But why wouldn't she? She had no reason to suspect otherwise. Now she had misgivings and even more questions to ask him when she returned. No one with even the slightest business acumen could have made the decisions Mr. Anderson made.

Hannah squashed her plans for a meeting between the General Managers and Corporate. She after all wanted to respect Naboth's decision to hold off until she returned.

She did her best not to sound irritated when she spoke with him, questioning his decision. But isn't that what she was supposed to do, stand her ground? Nevertheless, she conceded when he suggested she allow him to investigate the matter himself upon receiving her full report. But it wasn't his executive decision that bothered her, as much as it was the undercurrent tone of evasiveness she felt.

· · · ·

The flight home was mixed with aggravation and dejection. Hannah couldn't understand Naboth's reaction to her report and suggestions. Despite everything as the car pulled into the main gate, Hannah felt a wave of euphoria. "Home, she whispered." Immediately she flushed with guilt, thinking, "I never thought I would regard any other place as home. Granmama and Uncle Ivey are home, it's all I've ever known. It's just that now I think of Naboth and Julius as family, and where family is, home is. Isn't it?

"I suppose someday I'll have my own place."

She smiled, thinking about living on her own, decorating her first place. "If things continue as they are financially, eventually I will move back to the city, after saving enough and buying an apartment. Making a mental note, she reminded herself to call Granmama knowing she'll be worried when she doesn't hear from Hannah at least weekly.

As the car pulled up to the front door, Hannah in her excitement, couldn't wait for Joseph. She opened the limo door and ran up the steps, letting herself in the front door, yelling like a high-spirited teen, "Naboth, Julius, I'm Home!"

Julius entered the hall, greeting her with a wide grin, "Hannah, good to have you back!"

"It's good to be home Julius. Does that mean you missed me?"

Julius turned his head to mask the obvious joy of seeing her. Yes, he had missed her. The house was too quiet in her absence.

"Don't start Hannah," Julius replied.

"All right," she said, laughing. "Where's Naboth?"

"In the library. He's expecting you."

"I'll bet he is," she thought to herself. Their last conversation hadn't ended very pleasant." "I thought he trusted me, trusted my decisions. Naboth has some explaining to do."

Hannah stood in the doorway of the library, waiting for Naboth to look up and notice her.

"Hannah! Why didn't you say something? Come in. Come, tell me all about your trip. Did you see any places of interest? Don't tell me you just worked?"

Naboth's genuine excitement overseeing Hannah dissolved the mounting irritation she had felt until seeing him. Hannah couldn't help but smile.

"Hi, Naboth, the trip was wonderful. I didn't think it was right to do anything but what I was sent to do, work."

"Hannah, you take life too seriously. The operative word here is balance."

"Look at the pot calling the kettle black. I mean that figuratively, she giggled.

They both laughed.

"So, Hannah, tell me: did you have any problems with anyone? The General Managers?"

"No, as a matter of fact, they were glad to see a representative from Corporate, someone who could finally answer their questions. They were being told to cut back on everything from new purchases to employees. Who would give such an order? Most all the stores have great potential. With some training, remodeling in some instances and…"

"Slow down, Hannah!" Naboth said.

"I know. I guess I get carried away at injustices. I feel for the people who are involved."

Naboth loved Hannah's passion smiling, thinking of how Julia had shown the same passion regarding a special cause. Once she too got started, there was no stopping her. He knew at this point; he could no longer keep Hannah in the dark about who he was and the history of Vineyard Corporation.

"Whew, I've never flown so much in my life. I'm so glad to be back on solid ground. Again," Hannah said.

"You must be exhausted. Tell you what. You go on up, shower, get some rest. We'll finish this later, and I'll explain our next project."

"I am tired, Naboth, brain tired. I wouldn't be able to comprehend very much at this point anyway. I want to know what you are going to do about that Anderson guy? I don't know why that name sounds familiar to me. I keep thinking I've heard it before but can't seem to place it. Ok, I'm out of here. Thank you Naboth."

"For What?"

"Trusting me, for giving me this opportunity. Trust between people is everything, and you trusted me with this project. Thanks."

As Hannah walked up the stairs, she felt her legs grow heavy. "Jet lag is the pits," she concluded, as her mind filled with thoughts of Granmama, the people she had met who were depending upon her, Naboth, and Anderson. "Why, in God's name, does that name sound so familiar?" Hannah opened the door to her room, slowly walked in and fell across the bed. Balling up in a fetal position, she immediately fell asleep.

Hannah felt something warm and soft gently laid over her. She tried to lift her head to acknowledge, but tiredness and sleep summoned her, lulling her back into much needed rest.

"How is she doing Julius?" Naboth asked as Julius came down the stairs.

"She's asleep, Sir. I have a feeling she'll be out for a while. You may not see her before tomorrow morning," Julius said as the two of them sat down at the foot of the staircase.

"Thank you, Julius, I have a lot of thinking to do."

"Are you going to tell her?" Julius asked, growing consciously aware of where they were sitting. Somehow sitting on the stairs in conversation brought about a common casual ambiance to their chance meeting as they discussed their dilemma.

"Yes, I just don't know how much," Naboth replied.

"I believe you can trust Hannah."

"You really think so, Julius? I want her to stay I need her to stay. There is so much more I can teach her and learn from her as well. I'm afraid she'll leave after learning the truth. She'll not want to work for the likes of me. I wasn't upfront with her. Deceitful at best, not telling her that I knew Roland Anderson.

"Well Sir, if you don't mind me saying, maybe this is what she needs."

"What do you mean?"

"I believe Hannah to be a young woman who hasn't gained much self-confidence. Oh, she's been to college. Got her degree. But to really believe in herself and her potential, I don't think she's there yet. She told me she left school for a semester, running from a problem. Perhaps the truth will determine what she's got in the way of courage and endurance. Where she's headed, if you don't mind my saying, isn't going to be a picnic."

"You think you know where she's headed, Julius?"

"Yes, she's smart, good head on her shoulders. She has the potential to go a long way, but she's going to need a lion's courage."

"Well maybe, as you say, this is a time of testing for her. Perhaps to see if she is Vineyard material."

"And, Sir?"

"Yes, Julius."

"It's time to bring Miss Sarah in too. You can trust her. By the way, she called today, and I invited her out for dinner. The Joseph' going to pick her up."

"Now, Julius…"

"No need to thank me, Sir."

"That is not what I was going…" Julius was already headed down the hall.

Naboth sat on the stairs feeling a bit outwitted by his very wise and dear friend. He was going to have to face not only Hannah but also explain everything to Sarah at the same time. "Damn Julius!" Naboth said, shaking his head in resignation and exasperation, he decided to go to his favorite place of meditation and reflection. The gardens, where he did his best thinking.

Julius watched his benefactor and best friend from the patio doors. He knew he was going to his and Julia's special place. They would go there when they needed to ponder over a problem. His shoulders seemed to be more stooped today. It pained Julius to think that his friend was growing older and would one day…

"I don't even want to approach that subject right now," Julius thought. "Anyway, who's to say I won't go first?"

Julius' plan was to return home to South Carolina. He owned some land there and planned to build a small cottage and spend the rest of his days fishing. He'd managed to save a nice little nest egg. "With just myself and perhaps, someone special," he thought, smiling, "I could live the rest of my days in pure comfort. Naboth has been kind to me. He has fulfilled the promise he'd made to Mama and then some. I couldn't ask for more."

Naboth sat, staring into the horizon, wondering what he could say to Hannah. He felt ashamed for deceiving her, keeping his identity a secret. He had to know if he could trust her. He also felt he had to protect her from Roland. Not knowing the complete story kept him apprehensive about how to proceed. She was so devastated when they first met. "I suppose, he thought, I didn't want her to think Roland was a representation of Vineyards character.

Naboth you old fool, you've allowed your fears and anxiety regarding Vineyard to cloud your judgment. You've always been able to at least trust Sarah. Sighing deeply, he continued with his contemplations.

There's nothing much if anything at all I've kept from Sarah, yet I've been deceptive with her too. I really convinced myself I had no one to confide in, that I had to figure everything out on my own. Julia was my confidant, he thought, can I trust Hannah the same?"

Chapter Seventeen

Julius was so lost in thought, the ringing of the phone, startled him. It was Joseph informing him that he was arriving with Sarah. Just as Julius arrived at the front door to greet Sarah, she was exciting the limo.

"Julius, how good to see you," she said, waving.

"And you as well, Miss Sarah. Did you have a pleasant trip?"

"Yes, I always enjoy the ride out here. It's been a while. I was so excited when Naboth asked me to join him. Where is he anyway?"

"He just came in from the garden he's gone upstairs to shower and change. He'll join you in the atrium for tea shortly.

"Thank you, Julius."

"Do you remember the way?"

"Yes, I believe so."

Sarah sat mesmerized by the beauty of the Garden. Julia had worked so hard planning, designing, and mapping out every plant and its place.

Sarah smiled as she remembered how frustrated the hired gardeners became with Julia. But… she knew what she wanted and how she wanted it— flowers, foliage, fountains, and statues. It was as if she knew she wouldn't be around and wanted to leave something of herself, a legacy. "The result leaves one breathless."

Sarah called to mind the countless magazine and newspaper articles from across the country about the garden. Laughing, Sarah pictured Julia in her garden hat and gloves, helping with the digging and planting, working right alongside the gardeners. She winced, remembering how Roland would argue with her, "that's why we hired a landscape architect." Nevertheless, she dismissed his inference, insisting on being a part of her creation. Nothing would be planted that had not been touched by her own hands. She made sure she was there when every flower, bush, plant, or tree arrived She was determined to be a part of its beginning.

"Beautiful, isn't it?"

Startled, Sarah turned, "Naboth!'

"No, don't get up," Naboth said, walking over to greet her. Naboth extended his hand procuring a kiss on the cheek, causing Sarah to blush. "It's so good to see you. Please forgive me for not contacting you sooner."

"There's nothing to forgive."

"Oh yes there is, as you will soon find out," Naboth said, sitting next to Sarah and telling her of Hannah and their chance meeting.

"Naboth, I can't believe that you felt you could not trust me enough to share this with me before now."

"I can't explain it, Sarah. Except there's been so much going on with Mr. Scott, Roland and..."

"Since we are confessing, interrupting Naboth' explanatory confession. I have something I need to say to you. Several months ago, Roland came to me, trying to get me to assist him in plotting against you."

"Sarah, he what! The bastard! Why didn't you say something?"

"Naboth, it was you who created this atmosphere of distrust. I didn't know what was going on with you. I can't explain why I kept it from you. I've struggled with it for months. Wondering myself as to why I hadn't told you. I suppose it was partly because you seemed to be preoccupied, I didn't want to add to your concerns. Also, I figured I could handle Roland."

"I guess, Naboth sighed resolutely, I deserved your uncertainty. My being so secretive didn't help the situation."

"So, where is she?"

"Who? Oh, you mean Hannah" She's sleeping, just flew in this morning from an assignment I had given her. She was exhausted. I want you to meet her, so you may have to spend the night."

"Won't that cause suspicion if I am out of the office tomorrow?"

"Call in sick."

"I haven't called in sick in the forty years I've worked for you."

"Then it's about time, don't you think?"

"What about Mr. Scott? Has he come up with anything yet?"

"No, but he's close. His research has taken him to Holland. I haven't heard anything from him since he went there."

"Holland?"

"Yes."

"Naboth, what or who are you trying to find?"

"An heir, Sarah, an heir worthy of the Vineyard.

"But…"

"No buts, Sarah. My family, my ancestors have a long and rich heritage. We have come through much suffering and hardships. Our research has taken me as far back as the seventeen hundred and beyond. There is an ancient law that says the family inheritance must stay within the family. For me, it includes what Julia and I have built here and the business as well."

"But your niece and nephews, what…?"

"If I give it to Saul or Sylvia, I may as well hand it over to Roland. David…well…he's not like the rest. They would chew him up and spit him out. He's soft like his mother. No, I must find someone who has the chutzpah, the fortitude, to take over Vineyard, someone who believes in "tzedakh.""

"What is that Naboth?"

"It just means tradition Sarah. A tradition of kindness. I don't expect Sylvia, Saul, or Roland to fulfill or respect any of the traditions and principles Julia and I founded this business upon. But I must continue to hope that through my research, I will find someone to fill my place after I am gone."

"So, where does Hannah fit in?"

"I just want to train and mentor her, perhaps find her a place at Vineyard. She's good, Sarah. She'll be an asset to the company. I realize this may sound crazy to you, Sarah. I trust you to keep everything I've told you until I am ready to reveal it in my own time."

Sarah dropped her head in thought. Not knowing what to think.

Wondering, "Who is this young woman? How did she capture Naboth's heart so quickly? What kind of hold does she have on him that he would come to such a conclusion? Wouldn't Roland have hired her, if she was as qualified as Naboth believed? This is too much for me to absorb."

"Sarah? Can I trust you while I figure things out?" Naboth said, jolting Sarah out of her pre-occupation.

"Yes, of course, Sarah finally answered. Naboth, are you going to tell her?" Sarah asked.

"Not everything only that I will continue to tutor and mentor her and prepare her for a position at Vineyard. I don't know what capacity, as of yet. That's why I need your cooperation. I want things to remain as they are for now. Keep Roland out of the loop. I need to make sure she's completely on board. And some other things."

Sarah let out a sigh of relief, thinking, "He hasn't lost it completely. Maybe this will give him time to think things through. My God, he's only known this girl what, four, five months and he's ready to turn over major responsibilities to her, without telling anyone. That had to be the reason Roland has been so adamant about trying to reach Naboth. He said someone had gone behind his back. It must have been Hannah."

"Sarah, Sarah, are you, all right?" Naboth asked.

Sarah felt like she was in a fog. "Yes, yes, you're right, Naboth, mentor, train think about this, Naboth."

Julius didn't like the look on Sarah's face, thinking, "Was I wrong about her, God, I hope not." Julius observed Sarah's reaction. He didn't like what he saw. Would she turn on Naboth, when he made his final decision regarding Hannah?

Julius silently slipped back into the shadows of the adjoining room, heading back towards the kitchen to finish preparing dinner, still wondering if he had made a mistake.

He'd checked on Hannah again. At some point, she had risen, showered, and gone back to bed. He stood at the door of her room for a moment watching while she slept. He realized he was growing more attached to her. She was like his own daughter, an innate urge to protect was becoming more intense.

He had come to enjoy their times in the kitchen together with Hannah doing most of the talking, him listening. Their intimacy growing as she gradually revealed to him her private thoughts. It made him feel special. He would at any cost protect her from Roland, Sylvia, Saul, yes, he surmised, even Sarah.

If any of them could see the look on Julius' face at that moment, they would have no problem understanding his intentions.

"You put a lot on me today, Naboth," Sarah said.

"I'm sorry Sarah, I didn't mean to." Naboth was beginning to wonder if he and Julius had made a mistake by bringing Sarah in. Had he told her too much?"

Naboth rang the bell for summoning Julius, which he very seldom used.

When heard the bell, Julius knew it was Naboth's way of saying he was ready for Sarah to go. Something upset him.

Entering the room, Julius said, "Yes sir?"

"Julius, have you taken Sarah's bags upstairs yet?"

"Yes, they're in her room. Is there anything I can get you before you go up, Miss Sarah?"

"No, Julius, you are so efficient. Thanks. "Naboth, I'm going up to my room for a while. Julius, I look forward to dinner. I know it will be absolutely delicious."

"Yes Mam."

Naboth winked at Julius as he followed Sarah out of the atrium.

Getting back to his task in the kitchen, Julius was delighted when he entered to see (of all people) Hannah sitting at the breakfast bar.

"The dead arises," he chided.

"Yes, she does, and she's hungry. Can I have something to eat?" Hannah joked back.

"Sure, what would My Lady like?" Julius teased.

"Anything, food. Julius, I heard someone come upstairs. Do we have house guests?"

"It's Naboth's secretary from the office. They had some business to take care of, so he sent for her."

"Hannah shrugged. "Maybe it's about my findings. He said he was going to look into it."

"I don't know, Hannah, but don't you worry about that now. Rest your mind; there'll be time tomorrow for business discussions."

"I suppose you're right. So, what did you do while I was gone?"

. . . .

Sarah took her time preparing herself for dinner. She was tempted to go to Hannah's room, and chance a peek at the new woman in Naboth's life. Perhaps even get her alone so she could really find out who she was. But she resisted, showered and prepared to meet Naboth for dinner.

Naboth looked up as Sarah entered the dining room. His eyes couldn't help but express delight. She was beautiful. "Sarah, you look absolutely beautiful tonight."

Sarah hoped her look of surprise didn't show as she tried not to read more into his compliment than what it was, a simple compliment. Nonetheless, she took gratification in the momentary look of pleasure she saw in his eyes. "Thank you, Naboth. You're looking rather handsome yourself. Is Hannah joining us for dinner? Everything looks so good."

"No, last report she was still asleep. Remember she's been doing a lot of flying over the past couple of weeks," Naboth replied.

"Yes, I remember you doing the same in the early days. You would be worn out. I worried about you back then," she said.

"Those were the 'good old' days' weren't they?

"Yes, you were young and determined.

"Now, I'm old and stubborn."

Sarah couldn't help but laugh at the truth of Naboth's self-observation, commenting…, "That you are."

"Which one, old or stubborn?"

"I think a little of both," Sarah responded, still laughing.

The moment of laughter set the mood for the rest of the meal, making the time pass quickly.

"Naboth said, although I've enjoyed your company tonight. This old, stubborn man is going to turn in Sarah. Will you excuse me?"

"If you don't mind, I think I'll stay up awhile. I fell asleep earlier, so it's too soon for me. I couldn't go to sleep now even if I wanted to. The library sounds good. I haven't curled up with a good book in a long time. Perhaps Julius could bring me some tea?"

"I'll tell him for you on my way upstairs," Naboth said.

"Thank you, Naboth. Goodnight."

"Goodnight, Sarah."

As Naboth approached the kitchen, talking and laughter greeted him, could that be Hannah?" he thought.

"Hannah, you're up!" Naboth said, pleasantly surprised to see her.

"I got hungry, she laughed. Did you miss me at dinner?"

"Of course, I did."

"Well, "I know about your visitor. See what happens when my back is turned?" Hannah teased.

The three of them began to tease each other, bantering back and forth, relaxed and comfortable in the warmth of their evolving relationship with one another. Hannah and Julius were teasing Naboth, about romantic inclinations for Sarah.

Their conversation echoed down the hall as Sarah was heading for the library. Curiosity getting the best of her, she decided to go in the direction of the laughter.

No one noticed Sarah as she entered the kitchen where she found Naboth arm in arm with an astoundingly beautiful young woman. She felt a pang of envy as she watched Naboth laughing and joking with the woman as if he'd known her for years.

"Naboth, I thought you had gone to bed? Sarah said.

All eyes turned in her direction as the conversation came to an abrupt stop. "I was drawn by the laughter and a desire for some tea. I hope I'm not interrupting," Sarah spoke hesitantly.

"No, of course not, look whom I found, Hannah, Sarah, Sarah, Hannah. Naboth, initiating the introduction. Hannah and Julius were teaching me some slang. I think they were doing more laughing than teaching."

"Nice to meet you, Hannah," Sarah said, smiling.

"Nice meeting you too," Hannah replied.

My, she is absolutely, gorgeous, Sarah thought. "Her smile alone brightens up the room. I can see why Naboth would be smitten by her. But that's not the only attraction, I know Naboth better than that. It's her intellect, that would be the initial draw. I must get to know her.

"May I have some tea, Julius?" Sarah asked.

"Oh Julius, I forgot. That's why I came here in the first place. I was supposed to tell you to take Sarah some tea in the library. Sarah, my humblest apologies."

Naboth, Hannah, and Julius looked at each other and laughed. "Did I miss something?" Sarah wondered.

"Goodnight everyone," Hannah cheerfully acknowledged with a nod to each one as she started to leave."

"Goodnight, Hannah," Naboth replied. I'm right behind you."

Sarah turned to Julius. "I guess it's you and me, Julius. Join me?"

"Sure, why not."

As Julius was pouring the tea, Sarah asked. "So, what do you think about Hannah, Julius?"

"Maybe I should ask you the same question," Julius said, straining to keep from being curt. "I admit I had my doubts at first, but you need to get to know her before passing judgment as I did."

"I don't think I'm passing judgment, Julius. It's more concern for Naboth. He's getting his hopes built up in this girl. He's only known her for a few months."

"In all the years you've known Naboth, have you ever known him to be led by his emotions or to allow his emotions to cloud his judgment?" Julius queried.

"Never, but..."

"Then trust him on this, Sarah."

"I hope you're right, Julius."

"No, I hope I was right about you."

Julius' statement startled Sarah. It caused her to wonder what he meant.

"What do you mean, Julius?"

"Time will tell, Sara," Julius said, getting up to leave.

Chapter Eighteen

The dream was so vivid. Hannah was in a field, dressed as a field hand surrounded by other workers, both men, and women. Some were young, some old. They were harvesting a crop. It wasn't clear what kind of crop it was. As far as she could see, backs were bent, faces were taut and filled with pain. Perhaps slaves, she thought?

In the distance, she heard the low wail of a baby crying. But no one else seemed to take notice. A ghostly figure of a woman would fade in out of the scene, a stranger, yet somehow familiar. The woman kept motioning to her. "Don't you hear that," she asked the people around her. "Don't you hear the baby crying?"

"Finally, Hannah stopped her work and walked over to the strange woman asking, "What do you want?"

"Please," the woman said, "please help me find my baby."

"Where is your baby, Hannah asked, how did you lose it?"

Hannah wakened in a panic. Her heart beating rapidly as she struggled to catch her breath. In the dream she became fearful and frustrated in her search for the baby. Waking, Hannah became more agitated, trying to understand the dream' meaning. Finally, she resolved to try and sort it out at another time.

"I'll figure this out later, she said aloud, nervously laughing it off." She hurried and dressed her contemplation of the dream delayed her longer than she'd wanted. Causing her to be late in meeting Naboth and Sarah for breakfast.

Hannah was hesitant about meeting Sarah. "Sarah looked at me a little strange last night. I wonder what was on her mind." Maybe she was just surprised to see me. Perhaps Naboth hadn't told her I was here. Anyway, I'll get a chance to learn more about her today. We're both secretaries to Naboth. At least we have that in common.

"Good morning, Hannah," Naboth greeted her as she entered the room.

Naboth's warm smile and genuine greeting helped Hannah to relax, as she approached Naboth and Sarah, who had started eating without her.

"I thought it would be nice to have breakfast out here, Hannah. Hope you don't mind?"

"Good morning, Naboth. No, it's wonderful; you know how much I love the garden. Good morning to you too, Sarah."

"Good morning Hannah, Sarah responded nonchalantly, adding, "I hope you slept well last night."

"Yes, I did. Why do you ask?"

"I thought I heard a scream coming from your room. It was muffled but a scream none-the-less."

"Hannah?" Naboth asked with concern.

"It was nothing, just a bad dream, probably brought on by fatigue. I'm fine, really."

"I have something of great importance to discuss with you this morning, Hannah. Which is part of the reason Sarah' here. We're going to need Sarah's assistant."

"You sound serious," Hannah replied.

"I don't want to alarm you, Hannah, but it is serious. I am afraid it is also a little embarrassing for me. Nevertheless, I must tell you. Why don't we retire to the great room where everyone will be more comfortable?"

Hannah looked at Julius for some clue as to what was going on. But she couldn't determine whether he knew or not. He gave her no indication. "He's going to fire me," she thought. "Oh, God, how will I ever explain this to Granmama?"

The walk to the great room was teeming with silence. After they were all seated, Naboth turned to Hannah.

"Hannah, remember when we first met. The building where you had your job interview?"

"Yes."

"I own that building and many others."

"Well, I knew you had to be somebody important. I mean… really, look at this place and the vineyard."

"Hannah, listen. What I'm trying to say is… I am Vineyard Corporation."

Hannah paused, during the ensuing silence, Hannah reflected upon what she had just heard — allowing what Naboth had just said to sink in for a moment. Naboth, Sarah, and Julius watched her intently, warily anticipating some kind of reaction. Everyone was emotionally frozen in the moment.

As Hannah began to piece things together, she stood, "What?" Wait, wait. Ok, ok," she began taking deep breaths.

"She's hyperventilating," someone said.

"Hannah?"

"You mean you own Vineyard," she found herself screaming! But… but…the name of the Corp…

You've been helping me with a subsidiary of Vineyard, Hannah." Vineyard is the holding company of Family.

"But isn't that the place where I was interviewed by…what's his name…damn it. What's his name?"

"Anderson…?" Naboth added.

"Yes, that's it, Mr. Anderson Roland. Oh my God, oh my God, please tell me he's not the same person they were talking about while I was on my trip?"

"I'm afraid so, Hannah."

"I couldn't put the two together, because it was the name of the company that threw me off. I thought you were a chain or something. Or you just inherited wealth, I don't know. But I never put you with Vineyard and Roland Anderson," Hannah exclaimed becoming more and more agitated.

"You lied to me. All this time, you've been lying to me," Hannah sobbed, tears streaming down her face."

"I didn't lie to you, Hannah."

"You deceived me. That's even worse. How could you? Why? Do you realize how that man made me feel? You knew who he was and said nothing."

By this time, Hannah's emotions were out of control. She hated being out of control this way. Her words were coming in deep gulping breaths. I'm sorry, I need to get out," Hannah left, running down the hall and out into the garden.

"I'll go after her, Naboth. Don't worry," Julius said.

"Thank you, Julius. What have I done?"

Sarah couldn't stand to see the hurt in Naboth's eyes. She wanted to console him but didn't know how. "How dare she," she thought, "how ungrateful."

As if reading her mind, Naboth said, "Don't blame her, Sarah. I should have told her who I was. I had the opportunity to do so but didn't. It's a matter of trust. She trusted me, and believed I trusted her."

When Julius caught up with Hannah, she was sitting on the bench overlooking the vineyard.

"Hannah."

"What?"

"Can we talk?"

"Yea, I guess Julius."

"I think I know your usual response to conflict; He began."

"What do you mean?"

"Your normal reaction to situations that make you uncomfortable."

"And what is that?"

"One day while you were out, your grandmother called. She and I had quite a conversation."

"You talked to Granmama?"

"Yes."

"Granmama's always running her mouth."

"Watch it, girl. Don't disrespect your elders. I promised her that no matter what came your way, I wouldn't let you run anymore. And I…"

"I know, you keep your promises."

"You git'in smart, Girl?"

"How are you going to keep me from going anywhere? I'm grown, you know?"

"Then, this time act like it. Face your challenges. Stop running away from them."

"I'm scared, Julius. I've been smart practically all my life. Always did well in school, and I know I have the potential to do just about whatever I set my mind to do. But I'm scared."

"What are you afraid of?"

"I'm not sure. I keep having this dream about a baby."

"Huh? What baby?"

"Nothing. Never mind."

"Hannah, I don't know much about fear except what I experienced just before meeting Naboth, and I've had a few instances since then. But I can say this much; in all my experiences with fear, I realize as I keep moving forward in life, fear's grip becomes weaker and weaker. I know what I just said sounds simple, but I believe that as we continue to move forward, even though we're scared, fear realizes we're not going to quit. Fear eventually just gives up and let go. You get where you're supposed to be, wondering what took you so long to get there and why you were so afraid."

Hannah couldn't help but laugh at the simplicity of Julius' words. "Ok, ok, I get it. As usual, you're right."

As they both stood, she turned and faced Julius, giggling because she was looking at his chest. She took a few steps back, so she could look him in the eyes.

. "Remember Hannah, you didn't hear me say, "not" once, that it would be easy, life ain't like that. There will be good times, hard times, bad times."

"I know about the good times, but what's the difference between hard and bad? They both seem the same to me?"

"Well, hard times is like clay, when you leave it out too long, it becomes hard as a rock, and it seems like there's nothing you can do with it. All you do is add a little water to it and knead it until it's pliable, then you can make whatever you want of it. So, it is in life, hard times look bad on the surface, but all you have to do is add some water called tenacity and the kneading of determination then you can make anything you want of it."

"And bad times?"

"That's the hurting things in life, the part of life that runs deep in your soul, the ones you can't do anything about. Then you have to make a decision to either get through "it" or let "it" get you. Make you give up. Giving up, well…that's bad. Now let's go. That's enough of a lesson in Julius-ism."

Despite everything, that had happened, Hannah was able to smile, even laugh. Choosing to embrace the peace she'd gleaned from the truthfulness of Julius' simple wisdom.

They found Naboth and Sarah where they had left them. Hannah felt bad when she saw Naboth. It seemed she was either apologizing to him, or he was apologizing to her.

"Naboth," Naboth, looked up at her. "Please forgive me for blowing up the way I did. I'm so sorry."

"Come, Hannah, we must talk." "Naboth explained everything to Hannah, even Roland Anderson."

"You didn't trust me?"

"It wasn't a matter of trust, Hannah. I didn't know what Roland was up to and still don't. I thought I was protecting you, at least for the time being."

"I understand."

"So, I'll continue to train and mentor you. When you complete the Naboth school of business, you'll be able to run Vineyard if you have to."

"Ok, Naboth, Ok. But a job will suffice, Hannah said with a smile."

"Sarah are you with us?" Naboth asked?

The three of them, Naboth, Julius and Hannah, looked at Sarah, anticipating her response.

"Of course, Naboth, I just hope you know what you're doing."

"Be my ally at the office. As far as Roland is concerned, I don't know anything about what he tried to get you to do."

"Ok."

"Everything will continue as usual."

"But he'll know about my visiting the stores!" Hannah cried out.

"It's all right Hannah, I'll come up with an explanation. There are many ways I could have gotten that information. He's going to have to explain to the board why he made the decisions he made. I want to see how he'll get out of this."

Chapter Nineteen

Under a cloud of suspicion and mistrust, Naboth left the board room, fuming. "How did Roland get my signature on those documents?"

"Sarah, my office," Naboth ordered.

"Naboth, I swear to you I don't know how your signature got on those papers," Sarah exclaimed.

"He made me look like a fool. I can't believe he's so desperate that he's stooped to lies and deception. My God, even forgery! Is he that bent on taking over? And on top of everything else, he accused me of being senile."

"Well, not quite," Sarah offered.

"Well, he hinted at it!"

"Perhaps Naboth, you just don't remember signing."

"Sarah, don't you start. I remember everything I've signed since starting this company. And that incessant way he has of calling me 'old man'. I tell you, Sarah, Roland is getting desperate and will stop at nothing. This is getting serious."

"But, Naboth, no one took Roland seriously, especially the senility part."

"Maybe, maybe not. Even a seed of doubt is enough to cause the board to question my ability to run Vineyard."

"They would never," Sarah said appalled.

"Don't bet your life on it, Sarah. So, this is how he wants to play. I like your suggestion, Sarah. No more signing of documents with a stamp. My direct signature only, that's good. He won't be able to duplicate that. How many of those signature stamps do we have anyway?"

"Mine and yours were the only ones that I knew of," Sarah answered," but he might have ordered one behind our backs."

Roland went back to his office, still shaking with mixed emotions of anger and frustration, unsure of his next move.

Naboth had forced his hand with a card he wasn't entirely ready to play. He rushed back to his office internally berating himself for being so stupid, "fool," he spoke out loud," you practically accused him of being senile. Stupid, Stupid, Stupid! Too late, everything is out on the table. He knows now. I have no choice but to move forward with my plans. First, I need to find out who his consultant was, where she came from. Sarah would know. She *must* know.

Sarah flinched, the ringing of the phone startling her as she replayed in her mind the events in the board meeting. She still had her doubts regarding Hannah. She had her doubts about what Naboth was doing.

"Mr. Vanderhoten's office."

"Sarah? Roland is Naboth in?"

"No, he isn't. He's gone for the day."

"Good," he thought.

Cautious in his approach, Roland asked, "Is it possible, to have the number to the consultant he used for the report on the stores? She was so thorough I want to use her services. Ask her advice on some other projects."

Sarah was tempted to expose Hannah, forcing Naboth back to his senses, but she didn't. She had promised him she would trust his decisions.

"I'm afraid you're going to have to get that from Naboth, Roland. That was totally his project. He hired her I wasn't privy to that process."

"Liar," he thought: "Ok, thanks Sarah, I'll try to catch him at home."

"Yes."

Roland slammed the phone into its cradle, thinking "that was fruitless. I'll find out who the witch is if it's the last thing I do. Going behind my back was the worst thing Naboth could have done. He'll pay."

Chapter Twenty

The callous intentional charade that took place in the boardroom took its toll on Naboth. The pressure to maintain his composure in front of his directors and at the same time curb the overwhelming desire to grab Roland by the neck and...stop it Naboth. He's not worth the energy. And if you keep this up, a stroke. I wouldn't give him the pleasure," he concluded, continuing to talk himself down. "I've got to get out of here. I need to get home I must talk to Julius and Hannah. I don't know what Roland is up to. We may need to make plans for Hannah to get away for a while.

After notifying Joseph to meet him with the car, Naboth decided not to take the helicopter home. He needed the slow casual car ride through the countryside to help him relax. Naboth informed Sarah of his early departure and left through the secret passage.

He turned on the lights. The passage lit up like an airport runway. Naboth gasped did he see a figure at the end of the hall.

Blinking to adjust his eyes, he stared ahead focused and guarded. Cautiously moving forward, as he wrestled with the notion that someone other than himself knew of the passageway. No, it couldn't be. Only he and Julia knew of it. They swore each other to secrecy. Then they both conceded to informing Julius, Naboth trusted Julius with his life.

"You're tired Naboth," speaking out loud to console himself. "Your eyes are playing tricks on you."

Shaking off the suspicious, obsessive thoughts, Naboth picked up his pace in order to get to his private elevator as quickly as possible. "This has been one hell of a morning, he moaned."

Arriving at the elevator without incident, Naboth breathed a sigh of relief as the doors closed. He was glad to see Joseph as he stepped out.

"Good afternoon, Joseph."

"Good afternoon, Sir. Will you need to make any other stops?"

"No, let's just go home, Joseph. No hurry take your time. How's the weather?"

"It's unusually warm for this time of year."

"Then let's open the sunroof. I need to breathe some fresh air."

• • • •

"Damn, that was close. You've got to do better," Saul chided himself. The last thing you need is for Naboth to know you have access to the passageway.

Saul had squeezed in between two joists in the wall. For some reason, this part of the wall had been left unfinished. He watched as Naboth hurried by eyeing him with a malicious sneer playing at the corners of his mouth. "I could take the old man out without anyone knowing at least for a few days," Saul reflected for a moment. "It would certainly put an end to my current financial dilemma."

Being in the passage brought about unwelcomed memories of his mother. She had shown the passage to him, Sylvia and David one day as a surprise, swearing them to secrecy. It was one of her many games of adventure she played with them as children. He hadn't been back since he was a child. However, his desperate need for money had caused him to look for it again. It had been his way to get in and out of the building without being seen by Sarah or his father he loved the cloak and dagger adrenalin rush of it all. The secrecy excited him.

As the private elevator closed, the lights automatically went out. Saul paused, making sure Naboth had gone almost enjoying the darkness that enveloped him in a cocoon of blackness. It felt somehow safe. He could see nothing, and nothing and no one could see him.

Saul thought about his mother often. He'd loved her so much. Oh, how he missed her. Often without provocation or reason, she would walk up to him, pull him close, holding him against her swooning and cooing like a mother hen. Unbeknownst to her, the times when she would approach him to give him that special embrace...he needed it the most, as if she had read his mind. Tears filled his eyes as he moaned a deep resonating moan. A moan from unrequited grief.

Unaware of how much time had passed or how long he had been there. Saul finally moved, stepped out into the hall, groping his way to the elevator. Shaking himself, Saul spoke aloud, "Ok," he said, pushing the elevator button, smiling a sheepish grin, "Lets' get back to living."

Chapter Twenty-One

"What do you think, Julius?

"I think you're right. It may be the best thing at this point."

"Sarah said Roland has been quizzing her all day. To the point of harassment, insisting on knowing who Hannah is," Naboth said.

"Do you think…?"

"No, Julius, don't. I know she hasn't been in total agreement with us, but I trust Sarah. She'll come through."

"I hope so, Mr. Vanderhoten. It's just that Hannah's safety seems to be in jeopardy,

and we need to protect her."

"I think we're both on the same page with that one, Julius. So why don't we talk to Hannah, where is she?"

"She decided to take a tour of the vineyards. She left a little while ago with the caretaker. Mr. Vanderhoten, might I suggest…"

"Suggest what, Julius?"

"…that Hannah goes home for a visit. She's been talking about it as of late, she'd mentioned it several times. Perhaps this is a good time for her to go. At least until Roland calms down."

"Julius, that's an excellent idea."

．　．　．　．

Hannah was filled with cheerful adrenalin after her tour of the vineyards. Rushing into the house, "Julius!" Hannah called out. Bursting into the room as she finally located them, glowing with excitement.

"You should see… Naboth, I didn't know you were home. How did everything go?"

"Come in, Hannah. Have a seat."

"Uh oh, this doesn't sound good," Hannah said, reservedly.

After sharing with Hannah, the events of the morning, Naboth said, "So, what I want you to do is go home for a visit until this all blows over."

"Naboth, are you sure?" I mean…I don't mind staying."

"Yes, yes, I want you to go home. It's time. You haven't been home in over a year you need to go see your family.

Remember Hannah, family is important. We draw strength from family. Family keeps us grounded. Agreed?"

"Yes, agreed. I do miss Granmama and Uncle Ivey. But you and Julius are my family too Naboth."

"I know dear. But go home for a visit. It will do you good, Julius and I won't have to worry about you."

"And what about you, Naboth?"

"I'll be just fine. I want you to enjoy yourself, relax, see friends, go to your place of worship. The one you told me about. Where the people clap their hands and jump all over the place."

"You mean to church?"

"Yes, go to church."

"Hannah laughed. "I'm going to take you with me someday, Naboth. You are going to visit *my* church.

"I would love to. I want to see those people jumping all over the place and falling out "under the Power," as you say they do."

"When shall I leave?"

"The sooner, the better. When can you be ready?"

"What's today, Tuesday? I suppose by the weekend. I'll need to call, let them know I'm coming. Uncle Ivey can plan to pick me up at the airport. Granmama is going to have a fit. Is two weeks too long?"

"No, that's fine."

Hannah looked at Naboth and Julius. The two people next to granmama and Uncle Ivey, she loved most in the world. Every ounce of instinct she had said there was more to the situation than what Naboth and Julius were disclosing. Yet she knew whatever it was, they were thinking of her. So, she resolved to let it go, trust them. Secretly she was glad to be going home, excited even.

"Ok, get my ticket. Let me know the details so I can call home. I'll go upstairs and start packing,"

Chapter Twenty-Two

As Hannah grabbed her luggage from the carousel, she grew more and more excited, anticipating seeing her Uncle. Exiting out of the baggage area through the arrival door, she saw her Uncle pulling up in the old familiar blue pickup. She felt like a kid as she yelled out to him, "Uncle Ivey!"

Walking around the front of the truck, He smiled as she ran into his arms, greeting her with one of his tremendous hugs. Boy did she miss those hugs.

Hannah couldn't believe that her uncle, in his late sixties, could still look as good as he did. Arms and chest still muscular, average height and s-o-o handsome. She was amazed that some woman hadn't grabbed him up by now. Granmama didn't agree with his being so affectionate, but he dismissed it and hugged Hannah anyway. Contrary to what Granmama tried to make it out to be, the hugs always felt warm, safe and protective.

"You are looking g-o-o-d, Unc, Hannah sung out good like a song, teasing her uncle. How are you?"

"Oh, fair-ta-midlin'," he said.

Hannah laughed. Some things never changed she was glad they didn't.

Hannah chattered away as Uncle Ivey placed her luggage in the back of the pickup. He asked her if she was moving or just visiting. She stopped talking long enough for him to get in the truck then started all over again. As he pulled away from the curb, she asked one question after another about the folks in the neighborhood, the town. Her uncle, in his slow casual way, answered as much and as best he could.

As they began to come to the more rural area of the ride, Hannah became quieter more contemplative. She wanted to allow herself to experience this part of the way home in serene wonderment and silence.

Ivey eyed her every now and then just to make sure she was all right, not wanting to disrupt her train of thought.

"Uncle Ivey, how's Granmama?" Hannah eventually asked.

"Oh, she's fine. Doc slowed her down some."

"What you mean, Unc?"

"Well, she had a mild heart attack and…"

"She had what?"

"Hold on, Girl. Didn't you hear me say 'mild'?"

"And you didn't call me?"

"She wouldn't let me. You know how your granmama is. She said you just started your new job and all. She didn't want you to know, she didn't want you to worry. Thank God she was with doc when it happened. She was at his office for a regular doctor's visit.

Doc checked her into the hospital for a couple of days, then let her come home with strict orders to take it easy."

"Of course, she didn't. I'll bet she started doing more than ever," Hannah grumbled.

Ivey looked at Hannah, as she looked back at him, and they began to laugh uproariously, till tears were streaming.

"That's your granmama."

"That's your sister."

As they pulled up to the house, Ivey turned to her and said, "Don't let on that I told you about her illness, Hannah. It's just between you and me; you hear?"

"All right, Unc.

Hannah exited the truck, paused, facing the house. Taking in the sights and sounds of the moment, lost in the past.

Remembering how she used to climb the white picket fence surrounding the house. Running in and out of the Oleander bushes, playing tag, hide-n-seek with the other kids in the neighborhood. She looked at the Bottle Brush Tree that stood in front of her bedroom window. It had swooshed her to sleep many a night as the wind blew through its branches.

Hannah stepped onto the concrete sidewalk with its cracks and lumps that led up to the front porch. It was here she had drawn many hopscotches and other chalky childlike pictures. The sidewalk ended at the expansive front porch, where she and her best friend Molly spent many evenings talking about boys and the fast girls in the neighborhood, whispering so Granmama wouldn't hear.

As Hannah opened the gate, a collie ran from around the side of the house barking profusely wagging his tail in greeting. "Collie come here boy," she called.

Hannah never could understand why Granmama would name a dog after its breed. Collie *was* a Collie. He looked just like Lassie on TV. He followed Hannah everywhere. They'd had many adventures together.

"Granmama, I'm here!" Hannah yelled, petting Collie.

"Well now, look at you. Don't you look like something out of one of them fancy magazines," Granmama coming out of the kitchen, greeted Hannah. Granmama had on one of her freshly starched aprons. I don't ever remember seeing granmama without an apron on, Hannah mused. Granmama was all of five foot two, but fiercely bold. She was medium brown complexioned, with long gray hair, she kept in a twist at the nape of her neck. Hannah used to love to watch her comb and brush it out every night. She never let it hang down except when she went to bed at night, which puzzled Hannah because it was so beautiful.

"Granmama, you must be cooking."

"I am. Got some people coming over to see you later. The Reverend and some other folks from the church."

"Ok."

"You look good, child, maybe a little too thin, but good."

"Thanks, Granmama. Uncle, I can take my luggage into my room."

"It's all right. I got it. Talk to your grandmamma," Ivey said, waving Hannah off.

"About what?" Hannah said under her breath. Then said aloud, "Granmama, Uncle Ivey told me about your heart attack."

"Not that!" Ivey yelled from the bedroom.

"Ivey runs his mouth too much," Granmama growled.

Hannah laughed, "Uh huh, got you back old man."

"I'm just fine," Granmama announced.

"Are you doing what the doctor told you?"

"You just don't worry yourself about what I'm doing, Miss Lady."

"Fine, Granmama," Hannah quipped, shaking her head as she headed for her room to freshen up before company arrived. As she passed her uncle, he whispered.

"Why you want to go tell your Granmama I told you? Now I'll never hear the end of it."

Hannah chuckled as her Uncle gave her a playful shove. As she entered her room, nostalgia hit her head on.

Everything was pretty much as she had left it. From the pictures on the wall to her high school yearbook on the nightstand, she could tell Granmama had cleaned up some. She could smell the Lysol. "Granmama certainly believed in Lysol," she said to herself laughing.

Hannah sat down on the end of the bed, surveying her surroundings, then sighed lying back. The breeze flowing in through the window felt good. Hannah drifted in and out of sleep, thinking about Naboth and Julius, granmama and Uncle Ivey.

. . . .

"Hi, Mattie, is she here?" Voices from the living room wakened Hannah. She jumped up, rushing to the bathroom to freshen up.

"Here she is, they all said in unison, each one giving expressions of, "Girl don't you look good and my how you've grown since the last time we saw you," causing Hannah to blush beneath the accolades that were being directed towards her.

"Hi Reverend Anderson, Mrs. Anderson," Hannah said, greeting them with hugs and kisses.

Granmama had her usual spread. You name it; it was on the table. She must have cooked all day: greens, cornbread dressing, chicken, yams, and potato salad. The table looked like a holiday feast instead of an ordinary Saturday evening.

"Go on, Girl, and eat. I've got to put some weight on you before you leave here. You are too thin."

"She looks good, Mattie," someone chimed in. "I like her size," someone else said.

Out of respect to Granmama, Hannah ate. It did taste good. After everyone's attention turned away from her, Hannah seized the opportunity to slip out and return to her room to finish unpacking. While staring out the window, she saw a car pull up and out stepped of all people, Molly.

Forgetting about granmama and her visitors, Hannah yelled out the window, "M-o-l-l-y, get in here, Girl." Hannah heard Molly's knock and greetings as she made her way to Hannah's room. For a moment they stood, eyeing each other; then like two schoolgirls they screamed and fell back side-by-side on the bed in kiddish laughter. Giggling and hugging each other like the two old school chums they'd always been. Their gleeful reunion must have been noisy, Granmama yelled out, for them to settle down.

"Girl, you look good. Look at you," Molly said appreciatively.

"Girl, if one more person says that to me, I'll scream," Hannah giggled."

"You do look good," Molly dared.

"And so, do you," Hannah said, smiling.

"A-w-w, I'm alright. Wait until Asah sees you."

"Hush, Asah is a married man," Hannah blushed.

"Uh huh, retorted Molly.

They looked at each other and laughed again.

"Hannah, I know you're going with me Saturday night."

"Saturday night? Where?"

"A party down at the American Legion. Come on, Hannah, you've got to go. I know you brought something to wear. You had to know we would party, after all the years of studying and now working. I know you need a break."

"Yea, Girl I do." Hannah paused for emphasis… then said, "I brought this bad black dress, girl, just in case, laughing, Hannah eagerly drew it from the closet."

"So, Saturday, around eight. Ok?"

"Ok."

Chapter Twenty-Three

Saturday couldn't come soon enough. Hannah didn't want to leave her room until it was time to go. She sat staring out the window, wondering when Molly would get there. It was already after nine.

Her dress was a little shorter than usual. She mentally prepared herself for granmamma's comments and disapproval. Hannah decided to wait, until the last minute, before leaving her room.

"Here she is finally," Hannah said in exasperation, just as Molly blew the horn.

Hannah grabbed her purse, headed out the door, yelling as she went, "Goodnight, Granmama. Good night, Uncle Ivey. Don't wait up."

"That dress is kind of short, don't you think?" Grandmama said.

"No, Granmama, it's just fine. See you."

"Humph!" Grandmama answered.

Hannah winked at her Uncle, ran down the steps to her waiting friend.

"Girl, we gon' party tonight!" Molly greeted.

Hannah smiled, "I need to, been tied up too long, girl."

Molly laughed, joking and teasing with Hannah as she drove.

Hannah and Molly's friendship was strange, to say the least. They were as different as night and day, yet they got along so well. "It's probably because we complement each other, Hannah speculated. "Molly walks on the wild side. I'm a little more reserved.

All in all, Molly' been a good friend. Nothing I've ever told her in confidence has come back to me." In this little town, I would have heard something by now. Hannah looked over at her friend and smiled.

. . . .

The hall was jumping when they arrived. As Hannah walked up to the door, she was greeted by longtime friends and acquaintances. Different ones yelled out to her, "Hey Hannah, good to see you." "You lookin' good girl. "Looks like being up North been good for you."

Hannah returned their greetings, enjoying being the center of attention. Responding with hugs, tolerant of a few drunken kisses, as she made her way inside.

The hall was filled with smoke from cigarettes. The smoke was hanging in a blue hue as it lingered around the colored lights that dotted the room. "Don't they know what cigarettes do to you?" Hannah sarcastically said to herself.

Molly brought Hannah a drink. Taking a big gulp, Hannah couldn't help expressing her surprise, "Molly, what is this?

Damn, Hannah, will you relax."

"I'll get my own," Hannah retorted. "Molly knows better she mumbled, walking over to the makeshift bar across the room, ordering another drink. Bill Williams was the bartender.

"Hi, Billy, can I have a coke, please?" "Hannah! How you doin' Baby girl?"

Hannah grinned. She liked Billy. As crazy as she'd seen him act toward others, he'd never gotten out of place with, nor disrespected her.

"I'm fine," she answered.

"I know that, but how are you?" Hannah laughed, deciding to linger and talk to Billy for a while. Catching up on all the neighborhood gossip. Billy heard and knew it all.

"It's getting hot in here. I think I'll step outside for a while."

"All right, Baby girl talk to you later," he said, wiping a glass.

Hannah moved towards the door, looking around for Molly as she went. Hannah spied Molly on the dance floor, doing what Molly do, dancing.

Hannah shook her head in resigned amazement. Stepped out into the fresh air away from all the smoke and heat. Breathing deeply, filling her lungs with much needed oxygen. She had started feeling a little woozy.

"I don't know if it was the drink Molly gave me, or breathing in all that smoke," she thought.

As Hannah stood out in the cool air, her head began to clear. She began walking, nowhere in particular. Stopping every now and then to have a conversation.

Some things and people never change," Hannah reflectively surmised.

"Maylene is still having babies." Hannah couldn't believe it. Maylene said she'd just given birth to her eighth. Dooey was still running the corner gas station. Dinah her eldest, was now a teacher at the local high school.

"How can people stay in the same place. Never leave or venture out, Hannah asked herself, seriously puzzled?"

Some of them she'd known all her life. They'd never left Hadaran and were now raising second, some third generations.

To her delight, for the most part, for all intent and purpose, they were decidedly content. Wow, it's amazing," she uttered almost out loud.

"Hey Hannah."

Hannah looked up to see Asah. "Asah, I was wondering if I would see you tonight. How are you?"

"Oh, I'm fair to midlin."

Hannah giggled to herself. Yea, she was right, some things never change.

"What's funny?" he asked.

"Nothing, just something you said."

"Where you going?"

"Nowhere in particular, I just wanted to get out of the hall, get some fresh air. It was getting a little crowded in there. I guess I'll go on home."

"Want a ride?"

"Sure, getting Molly to leave now would be like pulling teeth. Let her stay." Hannah said, climbing into the truck. "This is new isn't it?"

"Yea, thought I would move up in the world a little. So, how are things going for you up in New York?"

"Oh, fair to midlin."

Asah laughed at Hannah's attempt at using the old sayings. They both laughed, breaking what seemed to be an awkward moment between friends who hadn't seen each other for a while.

"So, you been ok, lady?"

"I guess so. Sometimes I think I am. And then, again, I wonder."

"You want to talk about it?"

"It's Granmama. I just wish she would understand some things about me. That's all."

Asah listened to Hannah, allowing her to vent. He knew she was still trying to deal with what had happened to her. Even though it's been five years, he would never forget that night as long as he lived.

Hannah had called him hysterical. He could hardly make out what she was saying. When he finally got to her, she was a mess, clothes all torn, black and blue, sure signs that she fought back. He knew she didn't just give in. She would've died first.

He had a hard time convincing her to tell her grandmother. She kept saying her grandmother would blame her for what happened. He finally talked her into going home and telling her grandmother and Ivey.

When she did, he was shocked at Miss Mattie's response. She just sat staring straight ahead, not looking at Hannah at all. Neither did she try to console her. It was the strangest thing to him. Finally, Ms. Mattie responded in a matter of fact way, "This too shall pass."

He still believed Ivey was the one who had beaten the boy within an inch of his life. Maurice left town soon after. No one had heard from him since.

"Asah! Are you even listening, damn!" Hannah broke, began crying uncontrollably. Asah pulled the truck over to the side of the road, grabbed her, pulling her close, allowing her to release the anguish and frustration.

"I know your grandmother can be distant sometimes Hannah," Asah said, consoling her. But I know Miss Mattie loves you. You're all she talks about."

He felt Hannah begin to relax in his arms. The anguished sobs were becoming deep breaths of relief. Holding her reminded him of their relationship after the rape.

He had separated from Hattie Mae. They'd spent a lot of time together back then. Going for rides sitting out by the lake fishing. Hannah didn't want to be around a lot of folks. She was too full of shame and guilt. She had been a virgin when it happened. He told her she still was. That what happened to her didn't count. He encouraged her to keep herself as if nothing had happened. As far as he knew, she had.

Hannah had a good name and reputation. Unlike some of the other girls her age around town. He, along with her uncle, intended for her to keep it.

Pulling herself away from Asah, Hannah began to apologize profusely, "Asah, I'm so sorry."

"Now, come on. You have nothing to be sorry for."

For a moment, Asah became nervous as he fumbled with the keys in the ignition. What he saw in Hannah's eyes disquieted him. She wasn't the young girl that he knew back then. The girl he shared innocent conversations and harmless moments with. What he saw was a grown woman. Desirable, vulnerable.

"I guess I better get you on home," he said, starting up the truck.

Neither one spoke for the rest of the drive. Upon arriving at her grandmother's house, Asah felt awkward. He sat staring straight ahead, finally saying...

"Good night, Hannah. It was good seeing you."

"Good night, Asah." Hannah said, getting out of the truck, slowly walking towards the house. She wanted to say something more. But the words wouldn't come. She hesitated with each step, struggling not to turn and look back.

It wasn't until she was safely in the house that she heard his truck pull away. She stood on the other side of the door for a moment to catch her breath. God, how she wanted him. She wanted him so bad. Walking towards her room, she began sparring with her conscience. Her relationship with Asah had to change. It was good she lived so far away.

There were things happening to her inside. Emotions and feelings, she'd never felt before were beginning to surface. Ever since the rape, she had shut down. Never allowing herself to feel any emotions equated with sex or love.

She secretly envied the girls at school when they talked about their relationships and latest boyfriends. She would always leave the room when they started talking.

Hannah had dated some in college. But as soon as the guys started getting too close, she would cut them off. She'd never had sex prior to the rape, she never had sex after. She hadn't felt much like it anyway. The guys in the dorm nick-named her "ice". It bothered her at first, but after a while, she learned to roll with the verbal punches.

Now emotions, feelings, sexual desires, everything was hitting her all at once. There were times when she felt in control. There were times when she wanted to scream at the top of her lungs.

God, she wished she had someone to talk to. Asah used to be that someone but now she wasn't so sure. Her feelings toward him were different.

While undressing, Hannah's thoughts began ricocheting and bouncing from one emotion to another. She crawled into bed, her eyes filling with tears as she emitted a litany of mournful moans, until finally falling into a fitful sleep.

Chapter Twenty-Four

"Hannah!" "Hannah!"

Hannah stirred, hearing faintly, her name being called.

"Hannah! Hannah! Girl, I know you hear me. What's wrong with you?"

"O-o—oh," Hannah groaned, remembering she was at home, then slowly recognizing Granmama's voice.

"Hannah!"

"If she calls my name one more time," Hannah thought, gritting her teeth then, answering, "yes granmama, I hear you."

"You getting up?"

"Yes Mam."

"You going to church this morning?"

"Yes Granmama."

"Well, you best be getting ready."

"Ok."

Hannah began making deliberate movements. Just enough to keep Granmama from saying anything. She felt as if she hadn't slept at all. Tossing and turning all night until finally drifting off to sleep at four a.m.

Going to church was the last thing she wanted to do this morning. To keep from having to explain to granmama, it was easier to just get up and go.

As Hannah entered the kitchen, the smell of frying bacon greeted her. Any other time it would have been a welcome aroma. Considering Granmama's Sunday morning breakfast, you would think grandmama was feeding a bunch of field hands, instead of just Hannah and Uncle Ivey.

"Good morning everyone," Hannah said, doing her best to sound cheerful.

"Good morning, Hannah, her Uncle chimed back. "You doing o.k. this morning?"

"Apparently not." Granmama piped in." "She didn't hear me after I called her, who knows how many times."

"Sorry, Granmama. I didn't sleep too well last night. I didn't fall asleep until four o'clock this morning."

"What's your problem?"

"I don't know, Granmama. Just couldn't sleep."

"Maybe you should see Doc Henry before you leave?"

"Yea maybe. I'll see."

Hannah thought, that's not such a bad idea. Recalling how gentle and kind he was after the rape. He had really made her feel comfortable despite everything. "Yes, perhaps I should go see him," she whispered.

Chapter Twenty-Five

"Hannah, there's nothing physically wrong with you that I can tell. I mean…I can run more extensive tests if you'd like. But I really don't think it's necessary."

"No. Thanks Doc."

"Hannah, may I ask you a question?"

"Yes, sure."

"Did you ever get help after the rape? You know, professional counseling?"

Hannah's head dropped. "No, no I didn't. Granmama said it was best to just put it behind us. She didn't think I needed it. I think she just wanted it to all go away. She acted like she was embarrassed."

"Well, I'm sure your grandmother meant well, but I am strongly suggesting you get some professional help. From what you've told me, I believe what's happening to you is more emotional and mental than physical. Of course, if you continue this way, it has the potential to turn into something physical, you know-stress and all."

"You think I'm crazy?"

"Doc Henry laughed. "No, Hannah, you're not crazy. It's just that you haven't allowed yourself to appropriately deal with this. Between the normal pubescent process as you grew up and the trauma of the rape, you've finally come to an emotional impasse, you need help to sort it all out."

"Molly said, I need a man."

Stifling a chuckle, Dr. Henry said, "I'm sure Molly thought she knew what she was talking about, but a man or having sex is not the answer, Hannah. You get involved with the *wrong* man you'll do even more damage to yourself emotionally. Sex is not to be taken lightly. Especially someone who has experienced what you have. Before you get caught up in a relationship with anyone, you need to build a relationship with Hannah."

"So, you really think I need to see a therapist. I mean that is what you are saying, isn't it? I better not tell Granmama; she will have a fit. She can't even say the word, 'rape'. To this day, she refers to what happened to me as 'the incident'."

"There's no need for your grandmother to know. I'm sure there are plenty to choose from back in New York, right?"

"Yes, thanks again Doctor Henry. At least now I know I'm not losing it."

"You're a long way from, how do you say it, 'losing it'. Take care of yourself, Hannah."

"I will. Better get on back. Granmama is probably on pins and needles waiting for me to get back and let her know what's going on."

The talk with Doc Henry helped. Hannah felt lighter as she left his office. The house was several blocks away, the walk home would give her time to contemplate her strategy of explanation to Granmama, which was no easy task.

Hannah spied Asah's truck sitting across the street. She looked around anxiously half hoping she wouldn't see him, still embarrassed about the previous night. "I'll wait and see him just before I leave to go back to New York. I'll say good-bye then," she thought.

Asah looked out the window of the café. Watching Hannah as she left Doc Henry's. It took all he had to keep from approaching her, all he could do was hope she was all right.

Arriving at her grandmother's house Hannah's steps became more labored. As she came through the door…

"Hannah, what did the doctor say?"

"Give me time to walk in the door, why don't you?" she mumbled under her breath. "He couldn't find anything physically wrong Granmama."

"What's that supposed to mean?"

"Nothing, it's just that physically I am as healthy as a horse."

"So, what is he saying, it's your mind?" Granmama said, hands on her hips.

"It's just that there are some things I need to work out; it's nothing for you to be concerned about."

"That's what I say about folk these days. First thing they want to say is somebody's crazy or need therapy. I watch them talk shows; I know what they're saying."

"It has nothing to do with being crazy, Granmama. It's just that, when you bottle up things for a long time, it starts to affect you emotionally. then a person may need help, to sort it all out."

"You plan on going to one of them therapist people?"

"Pl-e-a-se, granmama," Hannah gritted her teeth to hold back her growing irritation. "I'll work it out."

Granmama walked out of the room grumbling, "Ain't no crazy folks in *my* family. They may have done some crazy things, but they ain't crazy."

Hannah looked at her Uncle with raised eyebrows. "See, I knew she would react this way. No concern about me. Only about what folks gonna' say.

"What she just said, does it make sense to you? Folks done some crazy things, but they weren't crazy. Why does she think they did crazy things? Because they *'were'* crazy." Now I sound crazy trying to repeat and explain what *she* just said."

Ivey laughed, it became infectious, causing Hannah to laugh, changing her demeanor. "Uncle, I don't want to laugh right now, this is serious," Hannah said, trying hard to stifle the laughter that was working its way out.

"I know. I know, but you've got to find the humor in things sometimes Hannah. If you don't, you sho' nuff will go crazy."

Hearing the word 'crazy' repeated again sent Hannah into giggles. "I just thought, I mean, I thought she might think, perhaps feel, differently by now."

"Well Baby girl, you've gone off to college. Got a little more understanding about things. Your grandmamma…well, she hasn't moved an inch. That in itself, should tell you something."

"I guess you're right, Uncle Ivey," Hannah said, in between giggles, "I guess you're right."

"I don't know what you all in there laughing about, ain't nothing funny," Granmama yelled from another room. Ivey looked at Hannah and winked.

Chapter Twenty-Six

Dressing in comfortable clothes and shoes, Hannah decided to take a walk. She wanted to revisit the neighborhood, reclaim familiar streets where she grew up. The places she played, the secrets they held.

"Where are you going girl?" Ivey asked.

"Just taking a walk, Uncle. I'll be back soon."

"What she say Ivey?" Hannah heard granmama yell, from inside the house.

"Nothing, Mattie, she's just taking a walk, that's all."

Hannah strolled down the street. Contentment swirling around her like a wafting breeze. Every now and then a breeze would caress her, invoking a smile. Moments of brooding and melancholia jabbed at her thoughts. But the jovial greetings of familiar voices, smiling faces impeded brooding and melancholia. Surrounding her, in a cocoon of peace.

"Hey, Hannah, good to see you," Miss Marvela yelled from her porch.

"Missed seeing you. Heard you're doing really well," came from Mr. Pete.

They were all like family. Most of whom had a hand in sending her off to college. She would never forget them, couldn't if she tried.

Hannah concluded her walk into the center of town. What folks called "downtown." Downtown consisted of a post office, grocery store, local pool hall, café and Mr. Lee's Barbeque and Soul food restaurant. Everything familiar in its place. Except for a couple of new fast-food restaurants. Hadaran remained the same over the years. Constant, never losing its small-town character and charm. Personally, Hannah hoped it never would.

Hannah saw Asah at about the same time he saw her. Both waved at each other simultaneously.

"Hey, what are you doing walking?"

"Hi, Asah. I just wanted to make a last tour of the town. I decided to take a walk. It gives me a chance to say my hellos and goodbyes."

"Want a ride back?"

"Sure, why not?" I've gotten in my exercise for the day." As Hannah climbed in, she looked at Asah. "How are you doing, Asah?"

"I'm good, Hannah. I saw you the other day at Doc Henry's. Is everything ok?"

"Yes, I just wanted to get a much needed physical. It's been a few years, I wanted it to be someone I knew. Someone comfortable, familiar. I feel safe with Doc, you know since…anyway, that's why I was there."

Yea, I understand. So, you're ok, huh?"

"Just need to work out some personal stuff. Maybe someday I'll be able to tell you, all about it."

"When you're ready, Baby girl, I'll be here."

"I know, Asah, thanks."

"So, it's back to New York?"

"Well, not exactly. Actually, where I live is out of the City," Hannah said, describing the vineyard, mansion and the estate.

Asah glanced over at Hannah; he couldn't help but notice the glow on her face the passion in her voice as she described Naboth's Vineyard.

"Wow, that sounds great, Hannah. You know Naboth is a character in the Bible. An evil king and his wife, uh…uh…Jezebel, yea, that's it, Jezebel. Naboth wouldn't sell it to them because it was an inheritance from his family, so they killed him for it."

"That's right. I remember now. I learned that story in Sunday school. I kept wondering why his name sounded so familiar or where I knew it from. That's it, the story in the Old Testament.

"Naboth has been researching his family history. Maybe that's what he's trying to do?"

"What's that?" Asah asked.

"Find an heir," Hannah whispered mysteriously.

"You're leaving tomorrow?"

"Yeah, early flight. Uncle Ivey' driving me to the airport."

"So, this is good-bye."

"Yes, it is. I'm going to miss you, Asah."

"A-a-a-ah, you'll do just fine. Just continue doing good. Make us all proud."

"As Asah came to a stop at the house, Hannah reached for the handle, turning to get out. Asah reached for her hand and held it a moment.

"Love you, Hannah,"

"Getting out and closing the door, Hannah turned to Asah," Love you too. Bye."

Hannah took a deep breath as she opened the gate, turned to watch Asah's truck go down the road and turn.

"I need to pack," she thought as she entered the house.

From the side of the house, Ivey had been watching the scene unfold before him. He started to call out to Hannah, but the deep pensive look on her face stopped him. He'd always had his opinion about Hannah and Asah although he'd never said anything directly to her about it. For one thing at the time, he felt Asah was good for her after the situation with that boy. Now, he wasn't too sure. Nevertheless, he trusted Hannah to do what was right and Asah too.

Going straight to her room, Hannah was glad Granmama was out, giving her some alone time. Introspective time, to examine all the stuff that seemed to be flooding her mind, since returning home. It was as if coming home opened areas of her psyche that were closed, until now. Being home triggered a lot of memories, bringing to surface latent feelings and emotions.

"Granmama, Hannah spoke as if her grandmother was present. I just wished you could have said at least one positive thing to me while growing up. One word of encouragement would have sufficed. I mean, there were sometimes in my life I could have used something better than a 'this too shall pass'," Hannah said out loud to the empty house.

"Don't blame her too much, Hannah," Ivey said, appearing at the door.

Hannah let out a yelp, "Uncle Ivey, you scared me half to death! How did you know what I was thinking anyway?"

"Girl, I've been around you and your grandmother for most of her and all of your life. You really believe I don't know how you all think? You two been bump'n heads for years."

Hannah shook her head, "I know, you've been refereeing us forever. I've learned, you're the only one who can handle Mattie Hazel."

"She means well, Hannah. She really does. She's never wanted anything but the best for you, always. She just doesn't quite know how to express how she feels. She's from a different time, a different generation. Whenever she tries, it just comes out the opposite of what she really wants to say."

"Just one compliment or, I love you I mean..."

"Damn it, Hannah. Stop it... Just stop it!

Hannah looked up from folding her clothes, surprised at her Uncle's tone. As long as she'd known him, he'd never sounded so intense.

"I mean it! No more, enough! Are you going to leave here tomorrow, still carrying the same burdens you came here with?" You came home loaded down, so now you going to leave the same. Grow up. It's now or never!"

"Was it that noticeable?"

"Like an open book, her Uncle acknowledged.

Hannah, people can read you. You ain't hiding nothin', Girl. Look, your granmama comes from a whole different generation. They just don't do things the same way."

"But, Uncle Ivey, you've been different. You've encouraged me so much."

"And that isn't enough? Hannah, you can't expect everyone's going to respond to you the same way. If you do, you are in for a rude awakening child. You can't always depend on people to give you what you need cause when they don't, you got to be able, to give it to yourself. Whether it be love, encouragement, or whatever. Do you understand what I'm saying?"

"Yes Sir, I do. I really do. Uncle Ivey, do you think I'll get to the place where I won't need to be told that I'm good enough?"

"I'm sure of it, Honey. Absolutely you will," her Uncle said it with such conviction that it brought out a genuine smile from Hannah. She walked over to her Uncle threw her arms around him. He reciprocated with a hug that broke something inside her. Uncle Ivey's words reached her.

Naboth had been right. Coming home was a good idea. Her uncles' words produced a seed of courage. Hopefully the seed of courage would produce boldness, give her strength.

What was it that Julius had said? Hannah rehearsed his words, "where you're going, you're going to need it." "Wherever I'm going", Hannah whispered." "I'll rise to the challenge, I will.

Hannah couldn't wait to get back to Naboth.

Chapter Twenty-Seven

Hannah sat crossed legged on the living room sofa. She decided to call Naboth and Julius to confirm her flight information. Hannah was overcome with excitement as she dialed Naboth's number.

"Hello, Naboth?"

"Hannah, is that you?" how are you, my dear? How's everything at home?"

"Fine, I'll be leaving tomorrow. Naboth, I'm so sorry about what happened, that was so…"

"Stop, Hannah, there's no need for you to continue to apologize. I just want to know if you are all right. And understand why I made the decision not to reveal everything to you right away."

"I do, Naboth. How have things been since I've been gone?"

"Sarah said Roland is still trying to find out who you are. He's continued with his same old antics. Other than that, we're all anticipating your return. Although he probably won't admit it. Julius misses you too, more than any of us.

"I miss all of you too. Just wanted to confirm, my flight information."

After sharing her flight information, Hannah heard the front door opening and decided to cut short her conversation. "I'll see you tomorrow, Naboth."

"Yes, Hannah, can't wait for you to come home. Good-bye."

"Hi Granmama, how was your meeting?"

"As meetings go. Who were you talking to?"

"Naboth, I was giving him my flight information, so he could have the driver pick me up at the airport."

"Driver? Umph, you sure have gotten fancy: limousines living in mansions. Watch your step, Hannah."

An exasperated look came over Hannah. As she looked past Granmama at her Uncle, he just smiled and gave her a wink. Hannah smiled and pushed on, "Granmama, remember those pictures I asked you about?"

"Yes."

"Where are they?"

"Look in the bureau in my bedroom. They're in the top drawer in a box. What are you looking for anyway?"

"I just want to go through them. I like looking at all the old pictures hearing your stories about the people in them."

Ivey looked at Hannah, nodding approval.

"Please Granmama," Hannah said, moving up behind her grandmother hugging her around her neck. Pleading like a little child, begging for a special treat.

"Go get them pictures, Girl, quit worrying me."

An unexpected epiphany took over as Hannah began to see through her grandmother's demeanor. Hannah realized granmama's bark was worse than her bite. Hannah hurried to grandmama's room to get the pictures.

For the first time in her life, she cuddled up on the sofa next to her grandmother.

"Who is this, Granmama?"

Chapter Twenty-Eight

Making her way through the airport arriving at the exit, Hannah began looking for Joseph. She wanted help with her luggage. "Getting spoiled, aren't you girl? Yes," she thought, "I'm definitely getting used to this. Oh! There he is."

Hannah began to wave Joseph over to her direction.

"Miss Hannah, how are you? Did you have a pleasant trip?"

"Cut the act, Joseph." She said as they both laughed.

Hannah's relationship with Joseph had always been informal. Ever since he picked her up at the boarding house, they had become friends.

"Good to see you, Hannah."

"It's good to see you too, Joseph. How's everything at home?"

"W-e-l-l, let them tell you," Joseph said stiffly.

"Tell me what, Joseph? Joseph, Hannah insisted?"

Joseph just smiled sheepishly closed the limo door.

"Damn, Joseph, now I'll be wondering all the way home."

· · · ·

"Julius, what are you doing? Have you heard from Hannah yet?" Naboth asked.

"Bringing you breakfast sir. To your second question, Joseph just picked her up at the airport."

"Serve me where you've always served me, Julius."

"But, Sir, the doc...

"I know what Walter said, but I'm not an invalid-at least not yet. I promise I'll take it easy for the rest of the day. I'll have a nice relaxing visit with Hannah when she arrives."

Julius knew there was no arguing with Naboth. "Well, since I've already brought it to you, I'll go ahead and serve you here. I'll set up breakfast as usual tomorrow."

"Come on Man, spill it. You know it's killing you. I can see it all over your face, you want to say something."

"I was sure enough angry with Roland last night. I could have hurt him. Hurt him really bad, he practically threatened you."

"I know, Julius. He's getting desperate, desperate and dangerous."

"Well, I didn't know how to approach you. Him being family and all."

"You're my family Julius, the best friend a man could ever have. I owe you for what you did last night."

"Your debt was paid when you took me in Mr. Vanderhoten. Remember you saved my life; they were going to lynch me."

"It wasn't my purpose to bring you here as a servant Julius. I'm not sure what my intentions were, but it wasn't that.

As I've gotten to know you over the years, I want you to know you mean much more than a servant to me. I can genuinely say Julia felt the same about you. She told me so before her death."

"So, no more formalities. I feel we're both too old. Life is slipping away, so from now on, we are on a first name basis."

"Julius' eyebrows went up as he looked at his long-time employer. "But sir…"

"No 'buts' Julius. You laid your life on the line for me with Roland. I will never forget that. First names Julius."

"I'll try, Sir."

"Julius?"

"I mean, Naboth."

"Was that so hard?"

"No …Naboth. It's going to take some getting used to, sir."

Julius left the room, shaking his head. Smiling, he began whistling a little tune as he headed downstairs. "Yes," he thought, "this is a good day. Hannah's on her way home. Mr. Vanderhoten is all right. Yes, it's a good day indeed!"

Chapter Twenty-Nine

As the limo pulled into the circular driveway, Hannah's excitement mounted in her anticipation of seeing Naboth and Julius.

Although she loved Granmama and Uncle Ivey without a doubt, sometimes missing them like crazy. The realization of her new life was being manifested in ways she could never have imagined.

How could she have known she would grow so close to two perfect strangers she had met not so long ago.

She was no longer the old Hannah. Especially the Hannah her Uncle Ivey exposed and chastened; the wimpy, whining, I need to be validated Hannah. Despite it all, here she was. Living with two men in a strange place with no family close by, getting ready to embark on a new career.

"This is it," she concluded, "I'm really out here now, without a safety net. It's do, or die," Hannah said to herself, in a matter of fact way.

Walking through the door, she yelled, "Hey, you guys, I'm home!"

Julius was the first one to appear.

"Hannah, how are you? How was the trip?"

"Good, Julius, it was great. I can't wait to tell you all about it. But first I want to know what's been happening here."

"You've been talking to Joseph, haven't you?"

"He wouldn't give me any details, said I had to wait until I got home. I've been antsy ever since. The ride from the airport was not pleasant, at least emotionally anyway. Tell me Julius, what's going on."

"Hold on now. You just walked in the door. Get settled, Naboth and I both will tell you all about it over dinner."

"I have to wait until then?"

"Yes, you do."

"Joseph, you seeing to her bags?" Julius said, glaring at Joseph as he brought in Hannah's bags from the limo.

"I saw that look, Julius. Don't blame him. Where's Naboth?" Hannah said.

"He's upstairs in bed. He'll be down.

"In bed? Would someone please tell me wants going on! Hannah said, her voice escalating."

"I told you we would explain."

Before Julius could finish, Hannah was running up the stairs to Naboth's room.

"I may as well go on up too," he thought, following Hannah.

By the time Julius made it to Naboth's room, Hannah was sitting on the bed next to him.

"Come on in, Julius. Hannah and I were just talking about her visit home. Her friend, Molly, sounds like some character."

"Oh, she told me I had to wait, Julius said, with jealous jesting.

"All right, you two, tell me what happened," Hannah said as Julius and Naboth exchanged glances.

"Well, Roland kept trying to find out the identity of the person whom Naboth had sent to the stores," Julius started. When his patience ran out with Sarah at the office…

"He couldn't get anything from her," Naboth chimed in.

"He came out here to the house," Julius continued. "It was late when he came. We were pretty much settled in for the night. When the doorbell rang, I thought perhaps it was one of our neighbors in some sort of trouble."

"Yes, Naboth interrupted, Julius went to the door to find Roland drunk. I'm sorry Julius go ahead."

"Anyway, Julius said giving Naboth the eye, Roland demanded to see Naboth. I told him Naboth was in bed for the night asked him if he could wait and see him the following day. Of course, he wouldn't hear of it, demanding to see him right then. By that time, Naboth had been wakened by all the commotion came to the top of the stairs to ask Roland what he wanted."

Roland accused Naboth of going behind his back spying on him. Said Naboth was trying to get him fired. There were a lot of drunken accusations.

Finally, Naboth asked him to leave; there was no reasoning with him in his condition.

Naboth couldn't contain himself any longer… "Roland made the mistake of trying to get around Julius and come at me." "Julius blocked his way, told him that I had asked him to leave.

He took one look at Julius, knew Julius meant business. Finally, he backed down then left."

"Then how did you get hurt?" Hannah asked.

"Well he didn't really get hurt," Julius offered.

"What do you mean?"

"Naboth had a stroke, Hannah."

"A what?"

"Calm down, Hannah. It was very mild, Walter said…"

"Who is Walter?"

"Walter Sinclair, a longtime family friend and personal physician," Naboth answered.

"We tried to get him to go to the hospital Hannah, Julius added. But he wouldn't go. He's under Doctor's orders to take it easy. Ask me if he has."

"Come now Julius, it wasn't that serious, I didn't want the news to get out, that imbecile almost killed me. Walter said it was stress, brought on by a combination of everything that has been going on."

"And you guys kept this from me?" Hannah gushed.

"We didn't want to worry you, Hannah or…"

"Everyone wants to protect me," Hannah exclaimed, "Am I that fragile? Uncle Ivey and Granmama kept her illness from me too."

"Your grandmother is sick, Naboth and Julius said in unison."

"Granmama is fine, Hannah said sarcastically. She doesn't do what the doctor tells her to do either, eyeing Naboth as she spoke."

"We would have gotten in touch with you Hannah had we felt it necessary."

"Are you sure you're ok, Naboth?"

"Walter said he would look in on me in a few days. I'm fine."

"And Roland?"

"We're not sure, we're being cautious, staying in touch with Sarah," Naboth said.

"Does she know what happened?"

"Yes, I didn't want to make the mistake of keeping anything from her as I've done in the past. We thought it best to make her aware. She wasn't very happy about it at all. I asked her to take precautions also. We're all going to stay alert until we know what Roland is up to. The same goes for you too young lady."

Satisfied they were completely honest with her, Hannah said, "I'll let you get some rest Naboth, per doctor's orders. See you later at dinner," Hannah blew Naboth a kiss as she left the room.

Chapter Thirty

Hannah turned over on her back stretched her five-foot six frame the length of the huge bed, a lot bigger than the one she'd slept in at home. "Don't get too used to this," she reminded herself.

Remember, this is not permanent. As soon as you start working for Naboth at Vineyard along with the other executives, you are going to get your own place. Meanwhile, she thought I'm going to milk it for all it's worth.

M-m-m, I wonder if I can get Julius to make me one of his great omelets." With that in mind, she quickly jumped up dressed, hurried downstairs to look for Julius.

"Good morning Julius," Hannah said.

"Good morning, Hannah. You sound pretty cheerful this morning."

"I suppose I am. Can I ask you a favor?"

"You must want an omelet this morning."

Hannah screamed, "How did you know I was going to…

"You haven't asked in a while. I just figured it was coming."

Hannah couldn't help looking at Julius with amazement, and giggling, "Is Naboth coming down today?"

"I think he will. That bedroom is closing in on him by now. I'm surprised he's stayed in it as long as he has." "He's on the phone now with Scott."

"What's going on? Is everything all right?"

"As a matter of fact, I think it's good news. He's been out of the country, and apparently, he's found something."

"I hope so. I just hate to see Naboth continue to be disappointed. Not to mention the possibility of Mr. Scott's bilking him out of his money."

"I don't think so, Hannah. Something is in the making. If it is as expected, Naboth may be taking a trip."

"How long have you known this, Julius?"

"Not long after your return."

"When was I going to be told about all this?"

Julius laughed, "He'll let you in on it, Hannah. He just wanted to verify the information as true."

"You two are getting on my nerves with your secrets."

"Eat your omelet, Hannah."

"Food is not going to make up for this Julius, "Hannah continued to fuss teasingly. "I don't care how good it is.

"So, you've brought the search home, Scott? You've actually traced someone back to the States?" Naboth asked with bridled excitement.

"Yes, Sir, I'm booking a flight back home now. I'll call you when I arrive."

"Good Scott, good. Naboth couldn't hold back the growing excitement." When he hung up the phone, tears filled his eyes— an heir, the possibility of an heir. He could only hope.

Imagine a blood relative right here in this country. If only Julia were here. Even though she didn't completely believe in what he was doing, she never discouraged him. "This is for the both of us Julia," he whispered.

Chapter Thirty-One

"Who is this?" Hannah shouted! "Why are you saying these things?"

Julius was just arriving at the door to the library when he overheard Hannah. Julius rushed into the library. He didn't allow himself to get too far away from her these days.

"What's going on Hannah? Did you find out who it was?"

"No Julius, what he was saying was awful. It made me feel so ugly and dirty. Among other things, he called me a 'wench'. What's going on Julius?"

"What else did he say?"

"He said I was no better than a common whore."

Hannah had initially reacted in fear when the harassing calls first started, but lately, she was becoming angry, determined not to be intimidated by her tormentors.

"If the phone rings again, how about allowing me to answer Hannah?" Julius offered.

Hannah looked at Julius, resignedly said, "yes, but it's not because I'm afraid."

Julius chuckled,

"I know Hannah." Thinking, "Damn them. Now they're coming after her. The bastards. I'd better make some phone calls. I'm going to need help protecting Hannah."

The ringing of the phone jolted Julius.

Julius had been mentally poised and locked for battle. What seemed like months, had only been several weeks.

The calls started not long after Naboth left to meet with Mr. Scott. Julius and Hannah never knew when the calls would come. Sometimes early morning or late at night. Always the same belittling of Hannah. Name-calling, and racial slurs.

"Hello! Julius bellowed."

"Julius?"

"Oh, it's you Naboth. I'm sorry. I thought you were another one of those troublesome phone calls."

"They're still coming?"

"Yes, Hannah and I are at our wits' end."

"How is she holding out?"

"Like a trooper. The once scared little girl has become an angry, bold woman. I don't know what concerns me more, her being afraid or being angry."

Julius' lighthearted remark caused both to laugh, shaking loose the wall of tension surrounding their predicament.

They had been experiencing another side of Hannah they hadn't seen before. It was both comical and unsettling at the same time.

"How are you doing, did everything turn out as expected?" Julius asked.

"Julius, you're not going to believe it when I tell you. Neither will Hannah."

"You're going to make us wait, aren't you?"

"Yes, sorry old friend. I need to keep this under wraps until the very last minute. Can't even let you in on this one."

For Naboth to keep something from him, Julius knew it had to be serious. There wasn't very much Naboth held back from him. The mystery behind Naboth's search peaked Julius' curiosity even more.

"I respect your decision, but it doesn't mean I have to like it," Julius said.

"All right, Julius. I'll give you a call in the next couple of days to let you know when I'll be returning. Take care of Hannah, will you?"

"With my life."

Julius hung up the phone more puzzled. Then hurriedly picked it up again, dialing.

"Hello."

"Hey Man., I told you I would call if I needed you. Well, it's come down to the wire. I need your help to protect Hannah. It's getting crazy man. Roland is planning a move I know he is."

"Alright, call me with your flight information. I'll have the limo pick you all up at the airport. No, she doesn't have to know you're here. You can stay in the caretakers' cottage near the end of the vineyard until Naboth returns to straighten things out."

"Meanwhile, I'm concerned. Hannah's life is in danger. Thanks, see you when you get here."

Julius exhaled deeply, feeling better knowing he had secured Hannah's safety. Ever since Sylvia came to visit again, after meeting Hannah, things had gotten progressively worse.

"Naboth's folks are crazy," he concluded. "I don't know what to expect of them anymore.

Sylvia drilled Hannah like a sergeant then practically accused her of wanting her Uncle's money.

Don't they realize Naboth has made sure they are all set for life at least everyone but Roland.

Naboth's intentions have been, always were honest and sincere. He would fulfill his promise to his sister. What more do they want," he screamed out loud?

"Who are you talking to, Julius?" Hannah said, walking into the library just as he was completing his outburst."

"I was just thinking out loud."

"That was a pretty loud thought, Julius."

"Phones are finally quiet?" Hannah said, with a sigh.

"Yes, I'd rather they were ringing. At least I'd know what people were thinking. The silence bothers me more."

Julius, do you really think they'd try something?"

"Well, I believe they know Naboth is away. So, no telling what they may try. You just remember our plan if anything goes down."

"I'll remember. You hear from Naboth?"

"I just talked to him. He won't tell me anything. He said he would tell both of us when he returns."

"And you let him get away with that?"

"I suppose you could have done better?"

"Yes."

Julius responded with a cross-eyed look at Hannah.

They both laughed.

The evening continued without incident. When the phone didn't ring, even once, it was a welcome respite.

Julius and Hannah talked long into the night. She shared with him how she was raped in her Junior year of high school. Her struggles with her self-esteem, how everything seemed to come together, during her last trip home. Even the impasse between her and granmama,

Hannah finally came to terms with respecting her grandmothers' "old school" ideologies. She had her Uncle to thank for that.

After all is said and done, Hannah knew without a doubt, her grandmother loved her.

Before turning in for the night, Julius insisted, he and Hannah take another walk-through of their plan in case of any incidents. Hannah argued at first maintaining she already knew it by heart. Nevertheless, out of respect for Julius, she conceded.

Julius walked Hannah upstairs, checked her room. When he was satisfied, she would be safe, he said goodnight.

Julius had received a phone call earlier in the evening that his help had arrived. After settling in, he would meet with them later, without Hannah's knowledge, to confirm their contingency plans.

With Hannah settled in, Julius made his move. Leaving through the lanai, keeping in the shadows, Julius crossed over into the rose garden. Moving across the knoll, to the road leading to the caretaker's cottage at the south end of the vineyard.

Approaching the cottage, Julius hesitated before knocking. Listening to the voices inside. knocking, while at the same time entering, he greeted his guest.

"Hi fellas, I'm Julius."

Extending his hand, "Hello Julius, I'm Hannah's Uncle, Ivey. This here is a longtime family friend, Asah."

. . . .

The meeting had gone well. Other than being nervous about staying away from the house too long, Julius felt good about their plan.

Upon arriving back at the mansion, Julius encountered a dark shadowy figure. The figure moved across the front of the mansion heading toward the back of the house.

Immediately Julius dropped to his belly, flattening himself against the ground. Surprised he hadn't been spotted on his way to the front door. Running in a crouched position up the steps to the front door, he noticed the motion light didn't come on. Julius paused for a moment turning to make sure he was alone. As he fumbled nervously for his keys, he was glad, he decided to return by a different route.

Half falling, he stumbled through the door into the foyer, making his way to the stairs.

Midway he heard breaking glass echoing from the back of the mansion, but the alarm didn't go off, indicating someone had cut the wires. He had to get to Hannah.

Taking the stairs two at a time, Julius made his way to Hannah's room. Catching a glimpse of a figure at the end of the hall. Julius slipped into her room, quickly closing the door without a sound. Moving to Hannah's bedside, he whispered, "Hannah!"

Hannah woke startled. "Julius?"

Julius put his finger to her mouth, "Sh-s-s-sh, there's someone maybe more, in the house. Remember the plan?"

Hannah shook her head 'yes,' then reached under her pillow for the gun Julius had taught her to use.

"Get dressed quickly. I'm going to get you downstairs. When I do, you follow the plan to the letter. Do you understand Hannah? To the letter," Julius said under his breath.

"Yes, yes, she answered in a hoarse whisper.

Over the past few weeks, having bounced between sanity and paranoia. Hannah had the presence of mind to lay a set of clothing across a chair in case she had to move and dress quickly. Grabbing the clothes, she bolted for the adjoining bathroom dressed then met Julius at the bedroom door. Following Julius as close as possible, they soon arrived downstairs making their way to the kitchen.

After Julius got Hannah to the side door, he looked at her then pulled her close, holding her tight.

"Julius, I'll be all right. I promise," Hannah said through Julius' muffling hug.

"You run like the wind. Go where I told you. I'll meet you there later," he replied.

"What are you going to do, Julius?"

"Don't worry about me, Hannah. Just do as I tell you."

Julius stayed at the door until Hannah made it across the patio disappearing into the blackness of the garden.

Julius let out a curse under his breath. He couldn't make his warning phone call to the caretaker's cottage. The telephone wires had been cut.

He could only hope if Ivey and Asah didn't hear from him, they would somehow assume the rest and take action. He could only hope.

Infuriated Julius thought, "To hell with these people. I'm going to find out who has invaded my house," Julius headed back in the direction of the intruders.

Chapter Thirty-Two

Hannah ran for her life. Her thoughts turning to Julius, with unsettling concern. She had to get to the caretaker's cottage, tell them to go back help Julius.

He'd said he didn't know how many intruders were in the house, she feared for his life. "God," she prayed, "please don't let anything happen to him."

Suddenly the smell of smoke penetrated Hannah's nostrils. "What is that smell, she wondered? Looking up, Hannah noticed the stars were not visible. The sky was becoming ominously, darker, the scent of smoke more intense.

Spotting a water pipe sticking up out of the ground, Hannah placed one foot on the pipe and grabbed the wire that held the grapes up off the ground. Holding onto the wire, she pulled herself up.

Looking over the rows of vines. What Hannah saw was horrifying, the vineyard as far as she could see was on fire.

While Julius was playing a game of cat and mouse with the intruders, suddenly the odorous smell of smoke interrupted him. Running to an upstairs window, he looked out, rage mixed with panic begin to set in. The fools had set the vineyard on fire. "My God, my God," he thought. "Did Hannah make it through?" Please God, let her make it through."

Hannah dropped to her knees. For a moment she was frozen. Shocked unable to move panic setting in, wondering what to do next. "Which way is it moving?" she thought. "I need to figure out which way it's moving, then I'll know which way I should go.

She recalled the days when she went hunting with Uncle Ivey. She remembered him teaching her how to tell time by the sun, and its shadow and…and…Hannah's thoughts were moving rapidly, trying to get to the point of remembering how to determine which way the wind was blowing. As the information began to weave its way through her memory, she began to recall what he had taught her. She remembered thinking how old fashioned, unnecessary it was. Believing she would never use what he was trying to teach her. "Yes…yes… I remember, leaves," she yelled out. "Throw a leaf...leaves into the air." Hannah looked around for leaves that may have fallen from the vine, something that would blow in the wind. She remembered her uncle telling her that leaves wouldn't come straight down they would blow with the wind or look at the tops of trees.

The heat was getting closer. The smoke thicker, she didn't have much time. Quickly she grabbed a hand full of leaves tossing them high into the air, they drifted toward the north.

"Oh my God," she whispered, it'd headed straight towards me. "I've got to run north." Looking around her, Hannah realized she would have to run in between the vines and branches. Pulling off her jacket to cover her face, she started pushing her way through. At times they were so thick she could hardly get in-between; the branches tore at her arms and legs.

Finding it harder to breathe as the thick smoke and stifling heat grew ever close, Hannah dropped to her knees.

She began crawling, hoping the air would be more breathable, closer to the ground. All the while terrified the fire would overtake her.

· · · ·

The men gathered in the cottage smelled the acrid odor of smoke, Asah turned to Joseph and asked. "Man is that a usual smell?"

"Sometimes the gardener will burn shrubs and dead vines once in a while."

"Well I think I'll take a look anyway, Asah replied." Stepping outside of the cottage looking up Asah's heart skipped a beat thinking, that's too much smoke.

Grabbing a ladder lying next to the cottage, leaning it against the cottage wall, Asah quickly climbed up. As he arrived at the top of the cottage, he couldn't believe what he saw. A wall of fire the length of the vineyard. He began calling for Ivey and Joseph, "The vineyard is on fire! The vineyard's on fire."

Ivey and Joseph rushed outside, responding in unison, "What, what did you say?"

"We're on fire, man. And it's headed our way!" "We're sitting ducks, y'all. "We've got to dig a fire line!"

"There's some shovels in the shed," Joseph yelled back, running toward the storage shed.

The three men grabbed shovels and began digging a fire line as fast as they could around the cottage. They were hoping the wind would change in their favor sending the fire in another direction. Meanwhile, they would do what they could to keep from being burned alive.

"Ivey," Asah said with dread, Julius didn't call."

"I know. Either he didn't have time, or something happened to him."

"You think Hannah was already coming through, Asah asked, not really wanting to think about the answer." "If anything happens to her," Asah said, answering his own question, "I swear I'll kill whoever is responsible. You can bet my life on that."

Ivey and Joseph looked at each other then, toward their companion who had made the remark. The look on his face said everything, the men continued to dig in silence.

Hannah had been crawling for what seemed like an eternity. Fear wouldn't allow her to stand up. Her thoughts were elusive, dreamlike. She kept seeing the woman from her dreams beckoning to her, as if to say, don't give up, keep going. "Am I moving," she asked? Not knowing if the women was real or imagined. Suddenly the air around her began to change. She felt a welcome cool breeze stir around her. Cautiously she stood as the smoke began to clear. In the distance she could see the cottage, thank God, she had been moving in the right direction. Unknowingly she had reached the north road.

Hannah ran, sometimes stumbling, falling, gradually, making her way toward the cottage. She felt as if she was moving in slow motion. She began screaming in pitiable yelps for help. Her throat was burning hoarse from having inhaled so much smoke.

"Did you hear that?" Asah said to Ivey.

"Hear what, Man?" I didn't hear anything."

"Wait. Listen. I could swear I heard someone scream for help," Asah said.

The threesome stood still, waiting in anticipation, as the fire began to change its course, hoping...

"Look," Joseph screamed, it's Hannah!"

All three men ran towards her stumbling figure.

"Here, you get her head," Ivey said.

"No, Asah said, I've got her." When Asah picked her up, Hannah's body went limp as he carried her towards the cottage.

"Is she breathing," Ivey asked, with fearful and trembling voice.

Joseph pulled back the covers on the bed, "over here. Lay her on the bed."

"Is there any water?" Asah asked Joseph.

"Yes, I filled up a bucket just in case the fire damaged the supply."

"Her breathing is labored. She needs a doctor. She must've inhaled a lot of smoke."

"Julius…please, somebody help Julius," Hannah pleaded in a hoarse whisper.

"Hush, baby girl, don't talk," Ivey said, in soothing tones, tears filling his eyes.

"Julius, Hannah insisted. Please, he needs help," she gasped.

"Asah, you and Joseph go. I'll stay here with Hannah. Has anyone checked to see what's going on with the fire?" Ivey said.

Joseph said, "it's still moving away from us. I know this place like the back of my hand. I think I can get us through. We'll take the limo."

Hannah thought she heard familiar voices but couldn't quite make out their origin. Was it Uncle Ivey? Battling with uncertainty, she struggled to comprehend what was going on around her, trying to recognize the voices, she drifted in and out of consciousness.

Chapter Thirty-Three

Joseph turned off the car lights as they approached the driveway, stopping just before the front entrance so they could exit the car at a distance. As the two men slowly approached the front door, they found the house completely dark the door partially opened. As they entered, they heard agonized moans of someone in pain. Following the sounds, they came upon a man hogtied with some kind of cording.

"Yep, Julius has been here," Joseph, said with a smirk.

Gunshots rang out from upstairs. Asah and Joseph raced up the stairway, abruptly stopping at the top of the stairs. Julius was coming down the hall in their direction.

"You all right man," Joseph said, elated upon seeing Julius. "What was the shooting all about?"

"It's lying in the hall with a butt full of buckshot. He'll live," was Julius' nonchalant response.

Asah and Joseph laughed. Thrilled their friend was all right. But joyous victory soon turned to concern, as Julius got closer.

Joseph said, "Julius, you're hurt."

"I'm fine. "Please tell me Hannah got thru," both men looked at one another, worried."

Asah patted him on his shoulder, "She did Julius, she's at the cottage with Ivey, she needs a doctor."

"That's a lot of blood man."

"It's just a scratch, Joseph. One of them tried to get me with a knife."

"Naw, man, you need a doctor," Joseph said without hesitation.

"Yes, I agree," Asah echoed.

"Without any other response to their concerns, Julius said, "I've got to get to the emergency generator, we need some lights in here."

"Where is it?" Asah asked.

"I know where it is Joseph volunteered, Julius you rest."

Soon after the lights came on Joseph returned to the mansion. Asah was attending to Julius' wound.

"Man, you need a doctor."

"I know, take me to see Hannah please. I need to make sure she's alright."

· · · ·

The men arrived at the caretaker's cottage. Julius was out of the car before his companions could assist him, bursting through the door, seeing Naboth...

"Naboth? What...when did you get here?"

"Julius, Naboth cried out! Thank God, you're all right."

"But...Ju..."

Before Hannah could get his name out, Julius rushed to her side, followed closely by Asah.

"Try not to talk, Hannah. Save your breath. You've inhaled a lot of smoke," Naboth instructed.

"Uncle Ivey, Asah?" Hannah said, trying to rise."

"No, Hannah," they all said in unison.

"I don't understand, why are you all here?"

"Joseph is outside in the limo," Julius said, he'll transport us back to the house, we used the limo phone to call for help. Doc's on his way."

"Naboth, your hand is burned," Julius noticed.

"I'll be ok, Julius. It's Hannah I'm concerned about."

"Let's get her to the car," Julius agreed.

Julius lifted Hannah from the bed.

"Julius, you're in...before Asah could say injured, Julius had lifted Hannah and on his way out the door. Naboth and Ivey following close behind.

The ride back to the mansion was subdued, each one lost in his own thoughts.

Naboth smiled to himself, thinking how certain events in life, can unite total strangers. Bringing them together for a common cause. He was content in knowing, if anything happened to him, Hannah would not be alone.

Ivey struggled with his feelings toward Naboth. Although he didn't completely blame him for Hannah's situation, he couldn't help but feel that he held *some* responsibility. It was his family who tried to harm her. For that, he was angry.

"I don't know who that fool Roland Anderson is" Asah pondered, "but our paths better not ever cross."

Feelings of distress and worry were slowly dissipating. Julius was having a hard time dealing with the idea of almost losing Hannah. No matter how much he told himself he had no control over what happened in the vineyard, he couldn't help but succumb to the foreboding feelings of what if's, if something had happened to Hannah. He wouldn't be able to live with himself.

Chapter Thirty-Four

Julius, Ivey and Asah walked into the lanai from the direction of the flower garden. Naboth watched as the three men approached him.

"Naboth," Julius spoke first, "We took a tour of the vineyard, most of it's been destroyed, except for a small section everything is pretty much gone. A small portion of the flower garden was also destroyed."

"I don't know what they were thinking," Naboth spoke out, trying to make sense of it all. Could I have prevented this, perhaps compromised with Roland in some way?" he asked himself.

As if reading his mind, Julius consoled him, "Naboth there was no way you could have known or foreseen this happening in a million years."

"Well, plants can be replaced. I'm just glad all of you made it out safely and unharmed that is most important."

"I just spoke with the police, there's a nationwide manhunt for Roland. Saul and his partners are singing like parakeets. He claims it was all his father's idea, says he paid him and his friends to do this." "As far as I know, Sylvia and David were not involved, they're working on getting Saul an attorney." "Apparently no one was supposed to get hurt. Their purpose was to merely scare Hannah into leaving."

"If it were me, I'd let him rot in prison. I'm sorry, Naboth, but when I think about Hannah in the vineyard surrounded by all that fire...not to mention this is not Saul's first brush with the law. How many times have they gone down and bailed him out of one thing or the other? Saul hasn't had to pay for any of his shenanigans, do Sylvia and David really believe he's learned his lesson?" Julius asked.

"I don't know, Julius. Nevertheless, he's still their brother."

"By the way," Julius said, "Hannah's grandmother left Hadaran early this morning. She'll be arriving this evening."

"Good, will you prepare a room for her, Julius?"

"Yes, I'll make ready the one that adjoins Hannah's.

"Naboth?"

"Yes."

"Ivey and Asah said, whatever you need them to do to help put things back in order, they could stay on awhile to help out."

"Thanks, Julius. They're good men."

Chapter Thirty-Five

"No, Father," Sylvia adamantly insisted. "You went too far this time. Saul's in jail. Why can't you understand? He's looking at some serious time. What were you thinking? Do you know how embarrassing this is for David and me, or don't you care?"

Sylvia's tirade left her father with no space to interject his usual controlling guilt-laden remarks. It was Roland's way of coaxing her, to give in, to his demands.

"Are you saying you're not going to help me?" Roland asked.

"No, Father, I can't. I won't."

"You ungrateful witch!" Roland said vehemently.

"Fine, Father."

Sylvia hung up the phone, tears streaming. She vacillated between love and anger for her father. Sylvia feared for her brother's dilemma. the whole situation created feelings of hopelessness. Stirring up childhood memories, a longing for her mother.

Sylvia hated feeling susceptible to her fathers' manipulation

When it invaded her emotional space, she would either go shopping or find some charity event to take part in.

After her mother died, she had to fight for her place as a capable member of a family filled   with men, being the only female.

Her mother catered to the soft sensitive gentle side of her femininity, teaching her well the art of being a lady. Upon her mother's death, Sylvia had to recreate herself, seizing a strategic position within the family structure then maintaining it. She accomplished her goal perhaps too well. All of them, her father, and her brothers became dependent upon her, everyone, but her Uncle Naboth. Try as she might, she could never penetrate his emotional side as she had her brother's and her father. "Well…daddy, she thought, we learned to play games with each other. Her brothers on the other hand depended on her as the older sibling, whether major decisions, money, or just needing to talk, they came to her.

The magnitude of her situation grieved her beyond words. Her grief was a result of shame for her father. Grief and sadness for Saul, for David, for herself. She resolved to get through her dilemma anyway she could. She was determined to come out unscathed and back on top.

Sylvia wasn't in denial about the dirt she'd done mostly out of loyalty to her father. But arson, attempted murder…her father had gone too far. She'd like to think that she had some principals. David walked in as she was wiping away the last remnants of tears.

"Are you all right, Sis?"

"No, but I will be, David. Father doesn't give a damn about Saul; he's just trying to save his own neck. What did the attorney say?"

"He's going down tomorrow to see Saul, negotiate his bail. We may have to come up with some serious money, Sis."

"What else is new?"

"I'm sure they'll catch Father sooner or later."

"Yeah, right sooner or later."

Chapter Thirty-Six

Julius entered the library to inform Naboth that everyone had gathered. Waiting on him. Naboth's back was to the door, looking up as if in meditative prayer. Julius hated to disturb him. Just as he was about to announce his presence, Naboth turned.

"Is everyone ready, Julius?"

"Yes. They're all waiting for you, Naboth. I don't know about anyone else, but I can hardly contain myself, wondering what you found out."

"All in good time, my man, all in good time. Come let us go."

. . . .

All eyes were on Naboth and Julius as they entered the great room.

Naboth looked around at the people assembled before him considering his relationship with each one.

Sarah, his loyal friend and employee for some forty plus years, I stopped counting long ago. After a long heart to heart talk with Julius the other night I learned she's been in love with me for quite some time. Talk about an old fool. I think it's time for me to admit I need her just as much as she has desired me all these years.

"Julius, my true friend. His love and loyalty towards me, has never wavered. I don't know what I would have done these past years without him, especially since Julia's death.

"Hannah, a God send. There is no replacement for Julia but if there were, it would be Hannah without a doubt.

"Sylvia didn't come; I feel bad about that. Nevertheless, David's here, and I'm encouraged by his presence, for my sister's sake. I have lots of hope for him. As long as he doesn't allow others, to influence him. Which is my only concern for David why I must do, well…anyway.

"Hazel, Ivey and Asah, wonderful people, all solid as a rock. It's no wonder Hannah has the character and stamina she has. Look at her foundation," Naboth resolved ending his reflections.

"I guess you all are wondering why I've brought you here this morning. First, I want to introduce you to someone. Mr. Scott, come in here.

Folks this is Mr. Savian Scott, a private detective. I hired Mr. Scott some time ago to assist me in a project I was working on. It began initially as a hobby of sorts. But then it became a true passion more validated as the possibility of finding a family member became more real.

You see, for practically all our lives, Julia and I was under the impression that we were the last of our family line. However, by searching our family's history, I stumbled on an interesting limb of the family tree. That's when I brought in Mr. Scott. The more we searched, the more we found a growing possibility of other living relatives. Although there were times that my dear departed sister, and others I won't mention names withheld thought I was somewhat foolish and Mr. Scott could possibly be taking advantage of me or as some would say, 'ripping me off. At this statement, Mr. Scott cleared his throat amusing the group sitting around in rapt attention.

Naboth continued, "Well, as it stands, my search has not been in vain. It has taken Mr. Scott across this country and overseas. We have documented, infallible proof," Naboth paused intentionally to dramatize his next statement…   "You Hannah, and I are relatives."

"What?" Sarah gasped. "Naboth, are you sure?"

"Uncle," David asked in utter shock, "how did you come by this information?"

Hannah and Julius looked at each other, stunned.

Hannah's Uncle looked at his sister and yelled, "Mattie, it's from Grandmama Julia's side, isn't it? Remember the stories she used to tell us. There was something to those stories, after all he bellowed!"

"I'll just be damned," Julius said with reckless abandon, rearing back in laughter. Of all the things I was prepared to hear this morning."

Hannah sat awed open-mouthed, in raptured amazement.

"But…but…how, how?"

"You all want to hear it? It is divinely amazing! It all starts off with a set of twins, well actually before that, the twins are, what connects, Hannah and me.

Chapter Thirty-Seven

Jeshurun Panicked, "But Kathryn, I thought you weren't due for several more weeks. I don't understand."

"You can't always predict these things, Jeshurun. You've got to find a midwife. See if there's one on board. G-o-o-o," Kathryn wailed in between clenched teeth as another contraction wracked her petite body.

Jeshurun ran through the ship, pushing aside anyone and anything that stood in his path. He received a few hostile words from some of the crew as he pushed by them, racing his way to the captain's quarters. Bursting through the cabin door he found himself facing an embarrassed captain with one of the female slaves. Dropping his head, Jeshurun apologized profusely but remained.

"Captain Voorheis Sir, I'm sorry, but my wife…my wife she's in labor Sir. It's totally unexpected. She wasn't due for several more weeks. You can't tell about these things you know. Please Sir, is there a doctor on board…a midwife, someone? Please."

Jeshurun knew he was babbling, but he couldn't help it. He tried not to stare at the childlike girl cowering in the corner; instead, he shifted his gaze to Captain Voorheis who was nervously straightening his shirt and trousers.

"Boy!" he bellowed.

The cabin boy came rushing in. "Go fetch Mr. Hendrix quickly," he ordered. Turning to Jeshurun, he said, "Mr. Hendrix came on board with a servant girl. She might be able to assist you."

"Thank you, Captain Voorheis. Thank you" Jeshurun said, backing out of the cabin, "Thank you sir."

Disgusted after having come upon such a detestable sight. Jeshurun held back the sick feeling churning up from his stomach. He couldn't allow himself the liberty to emotionally debate the captain's moral values. His wife was getting ready to give birth to their first child. On his way back to his cabin, he came upon Mr. Hendrix with his servant.

"What is your name?" Jeshurun asked the young girl.

"My name is Clara, Sir." "Where is your wife? The cabin boy said you might need me to assist?"

"Are you experienced in these matters," Jeshurun asked nervously.

"Yes Sir, I am."

"Come, this way," Jeshurun motioned.

After examining Kathryn Clara said, "She's about ready to give birth Sir. I'll have to ask you to leave. Please."

Jeshurun was glad to be leaving. He couldn't take Kathryn's moans, punctuated by an occasional scream.

"Is it that bad, he wondered?"

Clara urged, "Push my Lady. This time push with all your might, Its coming. Keep going my Lady. There, you have it, a girl!"

Kathryn was a little disappointed, she'd hoped for a boy for Jeshurun's sake.

"But wait…Madam, there's…there's another, Clara announced.

"Another? Twins?" Kathryn gasped, disbelieving.

"Yes, give me one more good push madam.

Kathryn pushed with all her might, screaming in agony. For some reason, it felt like this one was tearing her apart.

"It's a boy!" Clara said.

Kathryn was elated. She had her girl and Jeshurun had his boy, what a wonderful gift to present to her husband.

"But, Madam," Clara hesitated.

"What?" Don't hold back, girl. Tell me."

"The boy, he is so…"

"So, what?"

"He's so dark, Mam. Your daughter, she is fair, skin like milk…your son…mam he is, he's darker. As dark, as night."

"Kathryn laughed, "He takes after my father whose skin is dark and smooth as glass. My son will be a great man someday. Its fine Clara don't worry."

"Yes, Mam," Clara said. But in her heart, she had great concern. Apparently, this poor soul had no idea what she was up against in this new world she was about to enter." Clara didn't know how to tell her.

Clara stepped out informing Jeshurun of the birth of his twins. Jeshurun couldn't believe his good fortune two at once. He became so jubilant he shook hands with everyone. Smiling laughing on one hand, crying the next.

Eventually, Jeshurun went back into the cabin to congratulate his wife, to see his children. When he saw his son, he was shocked, at a loss for words.

"What's wrong, Jeshurun? Is something wrong with him?"

"No…no…Kathryn," he stuttered.

"Then what is it? Tell me."

"I don't know how to say this Kathryn, but we can't keep our son."

"Can't keep him, have you taken leave of your senses Jeshurun?"

"Kathryn we can't, Jeshurun repeated."

"What do you mean, we can't keep him, Kathryn screamed. He's our son Jeshurun!"

"You don't understand Kathryn. This is a different world here. It's not like where we came from. People won't understand. Africans are slaves here."

"Do you forget so easily, so was my Father." I am the daughter of a slave Kathryn said vehemently."

"And it's unfortunate. We can't keep him. People will ask questions. We can't afford for them to find out."

"Find out what? That your wife has African blood flowing through her veins? Is that what you're afraid of, Jeshurun?"

"It's not like that, Kathryn."

"I will not give up my son. I can't let him go, I won't Jeshurun."

"It's not your decision. You will do as I say."

Kathryn looked at her son, then Jeshurun, then her son again. Images of her Father and her African ancestors found their way into her thoughts as if reminding her of her vow to her father. Her body convulsed with sobs of grief.

"Kathryn, I…"

Kathryn turned her head, the sight of Jeshurun sickened her. When she did finally speak her words were laced with venom.

"You are truly your father's son."

Jeshurun flinched at the words hurled at him by the woman he loved so much. He had given up everything for her. "She'll get over it," he thought. "Time will heal her pain she'll see I made the right decision."

"Send in the mid-wife," Kathryn said brusquely.

When Clara entered, Kathryn said, "You must take my son. Swear to me with an oath, that you will never let him forget who he is. Swear!" Kathryn screamed!

"I swear, my Lady," Clara said through grim tears. "I swear."

Kathryn searchingly looked Clara in her eyes. Searching for a light of trust and hope that she was committing her son into the hands of a worthy guardian. Her son's life depended on it.

"This is what you must tell him," Kathryn began to rehearse for Clara, her father's words regarding his people, their culture, and their ways.

Kathryn had Clara to repeat her word for word. She didn't want her to forget. "Don't worry Madam. I will teach him everything. I will help you keep your vow to your African father I will raise him as my own," Clara vowed.

Kathryn held her son for the last time whispering in his ear, "My son, your suffering will not be in vain. In this land where you are despised, you and your descendants will overcome becoming a great people, increasing in wealth and honor, I swear.

Kathryn kissed him, then handed him to Clara. "Take him and go." "Clara, Kathryn called out to her...

Clara paused at the door, "His name...his name is Samuel, after my father.

"And Samuel it will be, mam."

Jeshurun had paid Hendrix handsomely to allow Clara to take the boy. It didn't matter to Hendrix. He had gotten the better end of the deal another servant, he didn't have to pay for it.

Kathryn overcome with grief reached for her daughter, taking her in her arms, whispering in her ear...,

"You must never forget your brother I will see to it that you don't."

As the great ship neared the dock, Kathryn stood on deck at the rail with Jeshurun. She held Lena close as if to shield her. From exactly what, she was uncertain. Only that her intuition spoke of unseen danger, cruelty like she'd never known. What kind of place is this, to cause separation between a mother and her child, Kathryn thought, shivering?

"Are you cold, my dear?" Jeshurun asked.

"I'm fine Jeshurun," Kathryn 's response was indifferent and distant, as she stared blankly looking out over the horizon.

The sun began to rise, sending a red-orange glow across the eastern sky. It's beautiful glow and brilliance mocked Kathryn's ominous mood. Sighing deeply Kathryn vowed in her heart. Whatever I am to face in this God forsaken place…for how can, God be in a place so cruel? I will not allow it to overcome or conquer me. I will find you my son, I swear, I'll find you, she cried out, in her heart."

Chapter Thirty-Eight

The morning after Naboth's news, Hannah wakened to mixed feelings. Her heart said one thing, her mind another and vice versa.

After hearing all the facts, pouring over papers and documents all night with David and Julius, Hannah was mentally exhausted. Asah had remained with them. Hannah believed it was because Asah didn't trust David, he felt she still needed protecting. Everyone else including Naboth had turned in for the night.

Along with everything else that had happened, Naboth proposed to Sarah. "Wow! What an emotional day," Hannah thought.

Hannah lazily turned over in her bed. Meanwhile, she heard voices coming from the hallway outside her bedroom door. It felt pleasantly strange, to hear someone other than herself Julius or Naboth in the mansion that was ordinarily quiet. Most of the rooms were filled with granmama, Sarah, David, Uncle Ivey, Asah; it gave the mansion a holiday like atmosphere having so many people around. As a way of celebrating, Julius and granmama cooked a fabulous meal last night, "It's been wonderful. Hannah thought," smiling.

And yet there remained an unresolved feeling in Hannah's spirit. The recurring dream she'd been having had lessened in intensity as if the woman (she now believed to be Kathryn) were somewhat satisfied. The baby they were looking for Hannah believed was the other twin Samuel. Hannah wanted to know what happened to Samuel. She believed that is what Kathryn wanted her to do, find out about Samuel. "I promise you I will," she whispered aloud.

Feeling a sense of peace and resolution regarding what she needed to do. Hannah got up to shower, dress, join the others who were already up and about. Granmama wouldn't approve of her lying around anyway. 'Best be gettin' up,' granmama would always say.

• • • •

The camaraderie around the breakfast table on the lanai was joyous. One would not believe there had been dissension between them the day before. All of them Granmama, Uncle Ivey, Asah, Naboth, David, Sarah, talking animatedly with one another, as if they were old friends.

This is the scene that Hannah walked in on. As she entered the lanai, she was met with a chorus of greetings that caused her spirit to soar. Whatever doubts she'd had dissipated at that moment as she offered her 'good mornings' in return.

Walking towards them, Hannah considered the peculiarities of life, its times of despair, soaring high's, to its nondescript moments in between, now and then serendipitous pleasures. All a part of life's cycle of seasons to remind us that we're human. Not super, just human a reminder of how much we need one another, this Hannah concluded, as she joined her family at the table.

Chapter Thirty-Nine

Time passed, and with it, the vestiges of all that had been revealed.

Granmama and Uncle Ivey finally went back home, assured of Hannah's safety, that she was in good hands.

Asah and Julius had become good friends. Asah would come up every now and then to assist Julius in restoring the damage to Julia's garden. Julius asked Naboth to allow him to do it instead of hiring landscapers, who weren't familiar with the original plans. Julius wanted to restore it back to its original state as much as possible.

The workers were busy replanting the vineyard with Julius and David as overseers. The two of them had acquired a growing interest in the vineyard and winemaking. Julius was more out of the house than in. Because of their time spent together, he and David's relationship evolved into a protective bond, David for Julius, Julius for David, which pleased Naboth.

The authorities were still looking for Roland. Sylvia was making somewhat of an effort at being civil. The thought of Sylvia brought a wry smile to Hannah's lips. Saul well…doing time in prison.

"How time truly flies," Hannah thought, "Has it really been three years?"

"Hannah?" Naboth interrupted her musings.

Hannah turned away from the bay window overlooking the city. The sky was clear.

It grieved her to see Naboth in a wheelchair. The stroke had been hard on him. But Sarah was taking good care of him, she loved him so much.

"Hannah, Naboth continued, it's time dear."

Hannah walked over to Naboth, stooped down before him, cupped his face in her hands.

Naboth looked into the eyes of his cousin, his daughter, his co-laborer, she has been all of that and more, he thought.

At first, the decision making had been under his tutelage from home. Hannah's business acumen became so effective; there were days when she alone made the decisions. The board members would call hailing Naboth, for the results when all the time it had been Hannah.

Now it was time Naboth thought, decidedly. I am finally at peace. I can let go. The Vineyard is in good hands.

He had no doubt as to who should take over. But Hannah insisted on a family meeting, "Everyone she'd told him, "Must be on board."

Sylvia adamantly resisted the position of CEO. She said she wasn't cut out for the rigors of running a major corporation. She just wanted to be sure her assets were secure.

David gave Naboth his full support saying, "Uncle, after seeing Hannah take over during your illness and I have no doubt, regarding her ability to run Vineyard. I trust her completely. With your permission, I will stand as her legal advisor."

"I love you old man," Hannah said tenderly. I promise I will take care of what you and Julia have entrusted to me."

Reluctantly Hannah left Naboth. She felt she would not have him very much longer. Hannah wanted to spend as much time with him as possible. Her mood was somber. Yet there was an innate prophetic call, propelling her forward into purpose and destiny.

With her were the combined spirits of two nations and cultures, hers and Naboth's. As their relationship grew over the years, they realized they were one. One in shared human experiences of pain, suffering and shared victories. Naboth, Julia, Jeshurun, Kathryn, the twins, Samuel and Lena, Granmama, Uncle Ivey, all those who had gone before her preparing the path that she would now take.

As Hannah walked down the hall, her gait became steady, more self-assured. Hannah felt the presence of a warm cocoon of ancestral souls surround her. It dispelled the dark negativity that had been so prevalent in her life. She could hear the words of Kathryn's father, the African... the prophetic vision...

"I had a dream before coming to Racife of traveling to a distant land, seeing strange people, speaking a language I did not know. Now I am here. Since being here, I have been given yet another dream, still another land, where I saw my people, my ancestors, being treated with such cruelty, so much so I could not bear to watch. Their backs were bent; their heads were low, their bodies barely clothed. Suddenly, one by one, they began to rise above the cruelty, as they were rising, their garments began to change. They took on the appearance of those that we now serve. They were prosperous, wealthy, heads held high. Kathryn is taking our next generation to a place of honor and prosperity. This is her destiny, our destiny, is letting her go."

"We made it Kathryn, Hannah whispered, just before entering the board room."

All eyes were upon Hannah, as she walked to the front of the room stood at the head of the table. "Ladies and gentlemen," she said, "My name is Hannah Lowenstan…"